Closure

Marie McGaha

Closure | 2
Marie McGaha

Publishers Note:
This is a work of fiction. All names, characters, places, and events are the work of the author's imagination. Any resemblance to real persons, places, or events is coincidental.

DWB PUBLISHING
www.dancingwithbearpublishing.com

For all the ghosts that have
been laid to rest

Marie McGaha

"Well, if you told me you were
Drowning, I would not lend
A hand, I've seen your face
Before my friend, but I don't
Know if you know who I am,
Well, I was there and I saw
What you did, I saw it with
My own two eyes, so you can
Wipe off that grin,
I know where you've been
It's all been a pack of lies
I can feel it coming in the air to
night, Hold on
Well, I've been waiting for this moment
For all of my life..."
-Phil Collins, *In The Air Tonight*

~ One ~

Zachariah Ellison ducked under the yellow crime scene tape that surrounded the area where the victim had been found. He shook his head as he saw a rookie cop run behind one of the police vehicles and puke. Zach had puked at a crime scene once or twice as well, but it had been a long time ago, and he thought now that nothing bothered him anymore. He couldn't afford for it to. He'd always known he'd be a homicide detective, even before he'd become a cop, although he wasn't sure if he'd chosen it or if it had chosen him. Either way, he didn't think too much about it anymore. He just did his job.

No attempt had been made to hide the body, even though it had been left in a remote area of the mountains east of Albuquerque, New Mexico. The area was sparsely populated. The trees weren't dense in this particular part of the high desert, but hikers often trek-ked up this way. Whoever had left the body here obviously wanted it to be found, but they'd been careful about it. The group of hikers that had found the dead man was still shaken by the sight, and a couple of them looked pretty green as officers took their statements.

Zach walked around the body, looking it over with experienced eyes. He'd been a cop for twenty years, fifteen spent in homicide, and he'd seen everything there was to see. Or so he believed most of the time. Though it still never failed to amaze Zach at how depraved human beings truly were. He'd seen some crime scenes that made him shake his head, wondering just how someone had even thought up such ways to commit murder. And this crime scene was one of them.

The cops at the scene gave Zach a wide berth while he continued his slow perusal of the corpse. His hands were clasped behind his back, his head tilted to one side as if the angle would give him an advantage. He was impressed with this murder. He'd seen a lot of messy crime scenes that immediately told him if the murder had been committed in the heat of the moment, a crime of passion, a crime of hate, or a drug deal gone bad. But this scene was almost a pleasure to work as far as Zach was concerned. It was nice and tidy in spite of the hideous method used to kill the man.

This murder had not been committed in the heat of the moment—it had been planned to the tiniest detail. There was no heated rage in this one—no, this was cold rage that had deadly, calculated results. This was personal. The killer had known his victim, had planned the murder, probably for years before actually carrying out the plan. There would be no regret, no remorse on the part of whoever had committed the crime.

No—Zach shook his head and smiled almost imperceptibly—*whoever killed this man was proud of their work.*

Zach wasn't a profiler, but he'd been on the job long enough to be able to figure out a few things on his own, without bringing in a psychologist to do it for him. Whoever had killed this man was making a point, and the hatred he felt for the victim was a palpable entity hanging on the air.

The nude body had been hung spread eagle between two small but sturdy pine trees. Nylon ropes had left deep cuts in the wrists and ankles where the victim had struggled against them. The body had been disemboweled, probably while the victim was still alive. The neck was swollen with an ugly purplish-blue tint to it. Embedded in the folds of skin was a narrow leather band, and there were bruises and singed skin over the torso that looked as if a stun gun had been used. But the icing on this cake, the thing that really told Zach what the killer thought of his victim, was the man's penis protruding from his mouth. The skin had been peeled and was hanging below it, stiffening in the hot desert air.

"He really ticked somebody off," the detective mumbled aloud as he circled the body a second time, clicking off the hand-held tape recorder he'd been speaking into as he observed the scene of the crime. Shaking his head, he walked back toward his vehicle.

"Petrie," he called to another detective, "take care of the scene and don't let anyone near that body until the crime scene unit gets up here. I want you to contact me as soon as they have anything at all. When Pete gets here, tell him to call me as soon as he gets back to town. I want to be at the autopsy."

"No problem," Ron Petrie answered, and then began barking orders.

It was nearly full dark by the time Detective Zachariah Ellison slid behind the wheel of his black Chevy Avalanche. He started the engine and made a u-turn back down the hill. The terrain this far from town was rocky and there wasn't a paved road for two miles. In fact, the path he followed was hard-pressed to be called a road, since the rains had long ago washed out the tire paths and left ruts in their place. The Avalanche's headlights bounced hard up and down as Zach steered to the right, then hard to the left, trying to avoid major holes and rocks protruding from the ground, and tried to keep his spine from compressing as he hit another hole. At nearly forty-two years old, he kept himself in shape, but it had been a long night, and he'd just as soon be home in bed.

Looking at his watch, he groaned. He'd been on his way home after spending more than fourteen hours at his desk when he'd gotten the call about the body. Now darkness engulfed him. He knew he'd only get a few hours in the rack at this rate—at least he hoped for a few hours anyway.

Pulling into his driveway a short while later, he drove the half-mile to the ranch house and parked by the back steps. A half-grown black lab came running toward him.

"Hey, Earl," he said and gave the drooling animal a scratch. "Want a cookie?"

The dog trotted up the steps to the back door and waited for it to open, nearly tripping Zach in its hurry to be inside where he knew the cookies were kept. Zach took a bag of dog biscuits off the shelf from above the washing machine, went to the door again and opened it.

"C'mon Earl." He coaxed the dog back outside and Earl dutifully followed him down the steps.

"Be a gentleman, Earl." Zach held up the

treat and the dog sat back on his haunches, waited, then took the offering gently from his master's hand.

"Good boy." Zach patted Earl's head, and left him to eat his treat.

Inside, Zach went to the kitchen, hit the play button on the answering machine, and ran the tap to fill the coffee maker. The machine played back several messages as Zach kicked off his boots and walked to the bathroom where he stripped and turned the shower faucet. After he showered and shaved, he poured a cup of coffee. He took a couple of sips, then vacillated between fixing something to eat or just going to bed. Bed won.

~ * ~

Zach had lived alone for nearly seven years, the same amount of time he'd been married. But the years alone felt much longer than the years he'd had with his wife. He'd met Stacie one night after work when he and some of the guys had stopped by Wrangle's for a drink. A law student who'd taken a job waitressing part-time at the sports bar, she took his breath away. Her fire and gold hair was pulled back in a ponytail and those cool green eyes gave nothing away. Taking orders, she serv-ed drinks and food with equal efficiency. The flirting from some of the cops didn't seem to ruffle her feathers either. She was tall with legs that seemed to go on forever, an ass he could build fantasies on, a trim waist, and her breasts made his mouth water. Her skin was pale and creamy, her cheekbones defined and she had proper manners accentuated by a sweet southern drawl. It nearly drove him crazy.

He'd asked her out that first night and she flatly refused, but she did agree to go out with him. When she graduated from law school, he proposed again and she accepted. Passing the bar exam on the first try, she hired on with the District Attorney's office. Two years later they decided to start a family, but Stacie didn't get pregnant. After one particular visit to the doctor, Stacie received a phone call from the receptionist saying the doctor wanted to see her again the next afternoon. Sending her for more tests, his suspicions confirmed, he said she had a rare form of ovarian cancer that had metastasized and was spreading at a rapid rate.

After surgery and months of chemotherapy, she quit. Begging Zach to take her home, she signed herself out of the hospital against medical advice, and three weeks later she died in his arms in the home they'd shared.

The alarm sounded and he smacked it. *Five more minutes*, he mumbled, *gimme just five more minutes*. It had been a long time since he'd dreamed of Stacie and he wanted to hold on to her for just a few more minutes. In the months following her death, he'd dreamed of her often, and more than once, he'd awakened with her name on his lips, reaching for her in the darkness. Eventually, the dreams became fewer and farther apart, but he liked having dreams about her like the one he'd just had. He didn't want to let her go, and wished he could roll over and go back to sleep.

Instead, he stretched and yawned, scrubbed his hands over his face and padded into the bathroom. After washing his face, brushing his teeth, and combing his hair, he headed for the kitchen and poured a cup of the now stale coffee. Nuking it in the microwave for a minute heated it up, but did nothing for the taste. Finally, dressed in jeans, shirtsleeves, and a brown blazer, he shoved his sock feet into cowboy boots, then filled Earl's food dish on the way out.

"See ya later, boy," he said and scratched the dog's ears. Then he headed outside, got into his car and drove down the driveway.

Less than an hour later, Zach pulled into his parking slot in the underground garage, he took the elevator up to ground level, and was immediately assaulted by the media in the lobby. Mumbling a curse under his breath, he tried to avoid them. If there was anything he hated about his job, it was the press. No matter what a person said or did, it was wrong, and he'd learned over the years to say next to nothing for as long as possible.

The barrage of questions began along with the blinding lights of video cameras. "Have you identified the body yet?" "Do you have any suspects?" "Is it true this was a ritualistic sacrifice?" "Is a satanic cult involved?" They continued firing questions at him without giving him the chance to offer an answer, even if he'd been inclined to do so. Sensationalism made headlines, and this case was sensational enough without Zach giving the vultures an opportunity to twist his words, and make the department look inept.

"There are no statements at this time," he

said and continued pushing through the throng to the elevator. "When we know something, you'll be the first to know." The elevator door slid shut in front of him and Zach shoved his hands into his jeans pockets.

Yeah, they'll be the first to know all right, Zach thought to himself with a smirk. If they were, it wouldn't come from him. There were plenty of others in the department who loved being in front of the camera, and Zach didn't mind letting them.

"I want Petrie in here," he said to his secretary, Ellen, as he walked into his office. He heard her on the phone as he shut the door behind him.

Bringing him a cup of coffee and a box of donuts she picked up each morning from the little shop across the street—even though he'd never asked her to do it—Ellen set it on his desk and said, "Petrie's on his way, he's been down to see the M.E."

"Thanks," he mumbled as he bit into a donut.

Shuffling papers on his desk as he ate, he booted his computer, and then scrolled through his email messages. One was from Petrie asking him to let him know when he got in, he had news. Another one was from Pete telling him the autopsy of the victim's body would begin at eight. Zach deleted them all and finished the coffee and donut as Petrie knocked on the glass office wall. Zach waved him in.

"Whadda ya got?" he asked through the last bite of his donut.

"Nothing," Ron told him.

Zach inclined his head. "Your email said you had news."

"That's the news. I got nothin', not a fingerprint, not a stray hair, no fibers, no biologicals. Nothing that doesn't belong to the victim."

"Hmmm." Zach picked up another donut. "Anything on the vic?"

"Ran him through AFIS and he's got a record a mile long. Clarence Broom, age forty-five. He's been in and out of the California system since he was a juvenile. Mostly drug related thefts, burglaries, that sort of thing. Convicted of a rape and robbery back in eighty-seven, paroled in ninety-two, did a few more years in the latter part of the nineties, paroled again, but seemed to do all right after that. Had a job at a garage, showed up on time every day until last week when he didn't come in or call, and no one's heard from him since.

"He's been married three or four times, all of them divorced him. Seems he likes to knock his women around. No kids that anyone knows of. Parents are dead. Two brothers, one in prison, the other doesn't have anything to do with him. A sister in Texas, but she left home at seventeen and never looked back. We're going to dig some more. I sent Jeffers to California this afternoon, but I doubt he'll come up with anything more helpful."

"Get anything from VICAP?" Zach hoped the Violent Criminal Apprehension Program might have some information they would be able to use.

"Nope. Some general stuff, but nothing

indicating it's a serial."

Zach nodded wearily. "They got anything downstairs?"

"Not yet, but I'll go back down and check on it."

"Never mind, I'll go see for myself," he said as he pushed back from the desk and stood.

~ * ~

Zach pushed the double doors open and walked into the coroner's office. "Hey, Pete," he called out.

Pete looked up from the table where he was working. "Zach. Come to see what I've got on your body this morning?"

"Anything I don't already know?"

The M.E. shrugged. "He died sometime yesterday late afternoon, early evening. He hadn't eaten anything in a couple of days, and COD was asphyxiation... mostly." Pete loved it when he got the chance to screw with Zach a little bit.

Zach raised a brow. "What do you mean *mostly*?"

"Well, the leather band that was tied around his neck had been put there while it was wet so as it dried, it..."

"Shrank," Zach finished for him.

"Mmm, hmm," Pete said. "Which is why his neck was swollen and bruised, petechial hemorrhage in the eyes, etc. But when he was sliced from pubis to sternum he was still alive, though not for long. Between the two—and either would have killed him—he actually died from the gutting. His penis had been severed and shoved halfway down his throat prior to the leather thong being tied there. Though technically, he was going to die one of three ways, no matter what."

"Someone did not like this guy, did they?"

"I'd say, uh, no," Pete replied in an almost sarcastic tone.

"What do you think about the skin on the penis being peeled like that?"

Pete walked to a table and pulled back the sheet. Zach looked at Clarence Broom and walked completely around the table, taking it in from all sides.

Pete waited until Zach finished his perusal of the body before continuing. "I don't really know," he said with a shrug. "But it's an unusual touch, don't you think?"

Zach thought he caught the corner of Pete's mouth twitching. He ignored it. "And you didn't find any trace on him either?"

"There are burns on his skin most likely from a stun gun, but as far as any trace goes, there isn't any. Actually, I'd say after he was strung up, he was given a bath, washed off, sprayed down, something. Whatever may have been on his skin, or in his hair, was washed away. Even his fingernails were scraped. Whoever did this wanted him to be found, but they definitely aren't looking to be identified."

"Somebody knows what we look for, don't they?" Zach mused, almost to himself. "Maybe we should be looking for someone who knows police procedure. That really widens the search grid, doesn't it?"

Pete nodded. "It would seem so."

"Okay, Pete. Thanks. If you find anything

else..."

"You'll be the first to know," Pete finished the sentence.

Zach went back upstairs to his office, shuffled through the pile of paperwork and shook his head. He hated paperwork and since he'd become a senior detective, it seemed as if that was all he did anymore. Picking up his coffee cup, he took a drink. It was cold and he grimaced as he swallowed. Then he went to work, and worked through lunch, finishing reports, looking over others, and then he picked up the Broom file and opened it on the desk before him.

Pressing play on the small tape recorder he carried with him to crime scenes, he listened to his own voice as he spread out the crime scene photos that had been faxed over from CSU. He was particularly interested in why the penis had been peeled that way. It was obviously done prior to being severed. But why? It was a very personal act, not something a stranger would have done. The entire scene had *up close and personal* written all over it, and Zach was positive who- ever the perpetrator was, they'd been carrying around a lot of hatred for this man for a lot of years. This wasn't something they'd just gotten up one morning and decided to do. No, this was something they had been planning for some time, and if not actually planning it, they had given it a lot of thought.

And wasn't that where action began? In the mind, *thinking* about doing something?

Zach slid the photos around, picked them up one by one, examining each one closely. Using a magnifying glass, he looked carefully at each and every detail. Something was bothering him, niggling in the back of his mind but he couldn't quite pull it out into the open. He picked up the picture of the penis with the skin hanging from it. What could the victim have done to warrant such hatred? Was it his rape victim exacting revenge? A pound of flesh perhaps? Zach made a note on the yellow pad to remind himself to check out the possibility. Could a woman be the perpetrator in this case?

Not that it was unusual for a woman to commit crimes of passion, but women generally preferred cleaner methods of murder. There were a few cases of women who had shot their wayward lovers, and one woman in Texas had run her cheating husband over with her Mercedes— several times. Those were exceptions though. Most women who murdered used poison because it wasn't as messy. Others chose to hire someone else to do the deed for them, or convinced a lover to do it. In general, women did not like messy crime scenes or messy crimes. Perhaps that was why the body had been washed clean.

Was the murderer a woman?

He shook his head. The way the man had been killed didn't *look* as if a woman did it. It was just so savage, and Zach had a hard time envisioning a female committing a crime that way. He sighed heavily. If it was a woman, she had some guts.

Ellen stuck her head in the office door to let him know it was eight-thirty. Looking up briefly, he said gruffly, "Then go home."

"I'm gone," she said and shut the door.

~ * ~

Having worked as Zach's secretary for the past eight years, Ellen had gotten used to his short-tempered remarks. She knew he wasn't being mean, and didn't mean to be rude. He just did his job, and expected others to do theirs with equal efficiency. He also expected everyone to leave him the hell alone. He had a few friends on the force—Ron Petrie and Pete Stratford were his best friends—and he got along well with most everyone most all of the time, but when he was working, he could be a real bear. He appreciated Ellen for understanding.

More than twelve years older than Zach, Ellen had been married to the same man since she was seventeen, and had raised three sons, one of which was also a cop. She had four grand-children, and after her sons had left home, she'd taken a business course at the community college, and for the first time in her life, went to work outside of her home.

She loved her husband, her sons, her job, and her life. She was also very fond of Zach Ellison. She knew he didn't have any family, and since Stacie died, there'd been a sadness about him. She could see it in his eyes that he couldn't quite conceal behind his bad manners. But she loved him just as she loved her own boys, and she worried about him, too.

And speaking of his eyes, she hadn't failed to notice the brilliant blue of them. She was a woman after all. The other female employees at the precinct hadn't failed to notice, either, even though it appeared that Zach rarely, if ever, noticed there were women working all around him. Ellen had tried to assist several of them with getting a date with Zach but to no avail.

What woman wouldn't want to date a man like Zach? He had penetrating blue eyes and his face was quite handsome. He had thick, dark hair that always appeared to be in need of a barber. He had high cheekbones, a straight nose, full lips, and a cleft in his chin. He was over six feet tall, broad through the chest and shoulders. Ellen had seen him in the gym one day when all he was wearing was a pair of gym shorts and running shoes, and even though she thought of him in a maternal fashion, she wasn't dead after all. Frank would be getting a little more than chocolate cake for dessert when she got home. He worked out regularly, and the muscles in his legs and calves were well defined. His stomach was flat and he had the coveted six-pack that came from regular exercise.

~ * ~

Zach was deep in thought, jotting down notes on the yellow pad and didn't even look up when he heard the knock on the door glass. He just kept writing and waved whoever it was in with the other hand.

"Detective Ellison?"

The female voice had him looking up, and in one sweep he took her in—tall, blonde, brown eyes, sweet smile, nice legs.

"Yes?" He frowned briefly and wasn't sure if he was disturbed because of the way she looked or because she'd interrupted him.

"I'm Amy Logan, District Attorney's office," she said as she came forward with her hand extended.

He didn't stand but shook her hand across

the desk. "Nice to meet you, Amy. It's a little late for the D.A. What can I do for you?"

"I'm new in the office, so I pull the crap work," she said bluntly. "Cooper is interested in this murder case you're investigating, sent me over to see what's going on, make sure the evidence doesn't get screwed up so when you find the guy who did it, we can go for the death penalty."

He measured her for a few moments. She didn't flinch as he continued to stare into her eyes. He fought the urge to blast her for insinuating his department would screw up the evidence, although he wanted to badly. Instead he remained calm and coolly observed her before saying, "Since when does Cooper get involved with a case before there's even been an arrest?"

"Since he decided to run for the Governor's seat next fall," she said and grinned at him as she took a seat

"Shoulda known. That S.O.B. has been greasing things in that direction since my... since I've known him." He looked uncomfortably away.

"If I can be direct, Detective Ellison?"

"I doubt you could be any other way," he said, the corner of his mouth curving slightly. "And call me Zach."

"Okay, Zach." She smiled and didn't seem the least bit offended by him. "I know your wife used to work in the D.A.'s office, and I know she died young. I'm sorry for that, it must've been difficult for you, but we both have jobs to do, and it would help us both if we didn't have to skirt around certain subjects when we do have to work together."

He stared into her eyes, looked at her face, and a beautiful one it was, he decided. That mouth was made to kiss and be kissed. He felt a tug deep inside of him, one he hadn't felt in so many years he almost jumped at the realization it was still there.

"Ms. Logan..." he began.

"Amy," she corrected.

He cleared his throat. "Amy, then. I keep my personal life personal, and I do my job very well. I expect no less from those I work with."

"Good," she said as she stood, "Then we understand one another." She laid a card on his desk. "You can call me at that number when you have anything to report." She turned and strode out the door.

Zach leaned back in his chair and watched her through the glass until she was out of sight. He laughed out loud then and said, "Guess I've been told."

~ Two ~

Zach slept like a rock that night and as much as he didn't want to, he rolled out of bed by seven the next morning. He didn't have to go in to the office but he had a ranch to run and there was paperwork to tend to. It seemed that was all he did anymore, paperwork at the office, paperwork at home. He hated paperwork.

He stumbled into the kitchen and made a pot of coffee, then stepped into the shower. He dressed, filled a huge travel mug with strong, black coffee to take with him and pushed the back door open with his elbow as he grabbed a doggie snack for Earl.

There were horses to feed and cattle as well, and though it wasn't a big place, it suited Zach's needs and it did require personal attention. Ranch hands took care of the stock all week, but when he had a day off from the force, so did they, and Zach took care of the animals himself. He'd built the house after Stacie died because he just couldn't stay in the one they'd bought together, and he didn't really like living in town anyway.

He'd lived where she had wanted to because he did whatever it took to make her happy. Not that she'd demanded a lot, he'd just been so in love with her that giving her what she wanted made him happy as well. But after her death there was no happiness in the house and too many reminders of her, so he'd packed the sentimental items off to storage. Most of the furniture and household items went to charity, and he'd priced the house to sell. It had taken less than three weeks to find a buyer.

Earl followed him into the barn and then hopped into the back of the old pickup truck when Zach fired up the engine. Driving through the pasture gate, he left it open, and made his way slowly down the path marked by the many previous trips made across the land. The cattle heard him coming and began making their way to the hay feeders. After parking the truck, he slipped on his leather gloves and bucked the bales of hay out of the bed of the truck and into the feeders. Standing back to watch the cattle come single file as they did every morning and every evening, he thought it must be nice to do nothing except graze in the sun all day and wait for someone to bring food. Of course, the downside would be that whole messy slaughtering business. Zach chuckled to himself and bucked another bale.

He jumped back into the truck and headed for the gate while Earl ran alongside, keeping easy pace, his tongue lolling out as he ran. Zach laughed at the dog and shouted out the window, encouraging him to keep up even as he brought the truck's speed up bit by bit until Earl was at a full-blown run. Going through the gate, he jump-ed out to shut it just as Earl barreled his way through. He rubbed the dog's ears and head and thumped him on the ribcage.

"Good dog," he told him and the dog seemed to give him a satisfied grin. "C'mon, you can ride the rest of the way," he said and snap-ped his fingers as he slid back under the wheel. Earl jumped over his lap and sat on the passenger side. After reaching the yard, they walked to the house together and Zach gave Earl a cookie, which Earl carried over to the lawn and laid down in the gentle morning sunlight to eat.

Zach went inside to fix breakfast when the phone began ringing. He considered not answering it but picked it up anyway.

"Hello, Zach? This is Amy Logan, District Attorney's office," the voice identified the person behind it.

"Yes, Amy, I haven't forgotten you since last night. What can I do for you?"

"I was just going over some notes, was wondering if you learned anything more I need to know? What can you tell me?"

He took a deep breath and exhaled slowly. "Well, Amy, I can tell you this is my day off and if you're going to call me at home, it better be for a reason other than your own curiosity."

"I just wanted—."

"I know, but like I said," he cut her off, "it's my day off. Come see me Monday during regular office hours, got it?"

"What time?"

"I don't care. And Amy?"

"Yes?"

"It's Saturday. Go home." He hung up the phone.

~ * ~

Amy Logan stared at the phone in her hand and set it back in the cradle. "Chauvanist," she said in a loud whisper.

She had heard how ill tempered the man was, but she had a job to do as well, didn't she? Oh, she'd see him Monday all right. She'd be waiting at his office door when he got in, and then they'd get this business settled. She had worked too long and too hard to get to where she was to have some overbearing, misogynistic, thick-headed excuse for a man telling her how to do her job.

Tapping the eraser of her pencil on the ink blotter on her desk while she fumed, she finally slid some files around, and raised the lid of her laptop to begin working on a case she was trying on Monday. Amy Logan was efficient, punctual, and well prepared. Her life hadn't always been that way but she'd worked long and hard to make herself, and her life, into something that matter-ed. She'd worked to put herself through law school, applied for every grant and scholarship available, and had even gotten a few of them. But she had put herself through law school on her own, unlike a lot of the other students who had rich daddies who forked over money, or were law school legacies following in their parents' foot-steps.

She'd come from hard-working parents who hadn't even finished high school, much less gone to college. They'd both worked at backbreaking jobs to raise two children and it had taken every dime just to keep food on the table and shoes on their feet. She'd been deter-mined from a young age to have more, to be more, to do more. It had been a long fight, but she graduated from high school, the first one in her family to do so, and she'd had to go to work right away because her parents simply couldn't afford to care for her anymore. Working as a cocktail waitress in seedy bars, and in some classy ones, she helped her parents pay the bills, but she knew it wouldn't get her anywhere. To Amy, it seemed like a never-ending vicious cycle she just couldn't break away from.

Taking drastic measures, she had broken away, had changed the course of her life... and that was all behind her now. No matter what she'd done in her past, it was buried so deep she was the only one who'd ever know. She wasn't going there. Nope, those things didn't matter anymore, she told herself and pushed the memories aside, shook her head and downed the last of her bottled water and went back to work.

She didn't know how long she'd been sitting there working on her cases, but her butt was numb and her legs ached, so she stood and walked around the office stretching, letting the blood circulate. When she sat back down and raised the lid on her laptop, she noticed the clock in the lower right hand corner and saw it was nearly seven.

She had a dinner date she was sure to be late for now.

Punching keys on her cell phone, Amy waited for an answer. "Sam? Amy. Yes, running just a few minutes late, but I'll be there in less than fifteen. Good... yes... okay. See you in a few." She pushed the end button, dropped the cell phone into her bag, shut down the computer and left the building.

Hurrying into the restaurant a short time later, she found Sam waving her over from a corner table. Samantha Jane Waters always wore the finest clothing to work, tailored suits from Ann Cline, Italian leather pumps, and always looked stunning with her manicured nails painted blood-red, and her auburn hair neatly coiffed. And now, seeing her sitting here at the restaurant on a Saturday evening wearing jeans, a tank top with a shirt over the top and a pair of white Skechers, Amy could only sigh. She envied women like that. The ones who looked stunning in rags, and could go from office to elegant in a single breath, who wore diamonds as easily as she wore faux pearls, which, of course, she never would.

Amy waved and made her way through the crowd, pulled out a chair and sat down. "Sorry, long day," she apologized.

"Never mind." Sam waved a slender hand. "I haven't been here long myself. I'd only just arrived when you called. So, did you meet Ellison?"

Amy nodded and took a swallow of water. "Last night."

"What do you think?"

"I think he borders on insufferable," she said with a frown, then ordered an apple martini from the waiter who appeared at her elbow.

Sam laughed. "He is that from time to time, but isn't it worth putting up with the rudeness just to be able to spend time looking at him?"

"I don't know, I guess he's all right," Amy said as she flipped open the menu.

"*All right*?" Sam leaned forward and lowered her voice. "I've been trying to get him to notice me since Stacie died."

"You knew his wife?"

"I did. Stacie was already here when I came to work. They were married before that of course, and I never saw two people more in love, but I thought after a while he'd at least start dating again. But it's been, what, seven years now? And I've not heard of him so much as having a drink with another woman."

"Maybe he's not over her. I'll have the scampi," she told the waiter when he returned with her drink. Then she handed him the menu.

"Me, too." Sam looked up at the waiter and smiled, and watched him walk away. "You know, no matter how many men I see, I compare them all to Zach Ellison. There's not another one built like him. And that thick, dark hair of his— man, I'd like to run my fingers through that," she said and then sighed. "And his eyes remind me of Paul Newman."

Amy shook her head and sipped her martini. "Well, he might be all that, but he's rude, condescending, overbearing, disagreeable, and I wish I didn't have to see him again."

"Maybe we can get Stanley to switch our cases," Sam said with a mischievous grin.

"Cooper? That old goat doesn't give a blue fig about anyone or anything other than his own aspirations. He's enough to make me want to switch sides."

Sam threw her head back and laughed. "You really call 'em like you see 'em don't you, Amy?"

"I just can't see doing it any other way."

Sam sobered a bit. "Just make sure you only say things like that away from the office and the people who work there. The walls have ears, but they also have wagging tongues and are more than happy to tattle. It's all politics in this office and everyone here is out for one thing: to promote themselves any way at all. So be very careful with what you say, okay?"

"I appreciate the advice, and I'll do my best to hold my tongue. It's not easy, and I was thinking of giving Zach Ellison a piece of my mind on Monday." They continued the conversation of small talk and shop talk until their orders arrived.

She moved her silverware so the waiter could set her dinner on the table. "Thank you," she said and smiled at him.

"Thank you," Sam said as her dinner was set before her. "Don't you have a case Monday morning?"

"I do, but not until ten. It's just pre-trial and they'll probably plead out. I wanted to see Zach first thing, since I have to talk to him about the hooker murder case anyway. He is going to testify, and I have to prepare him." She bit into a shrimp. "Although I'm sure he's done this so many times he'll not want any advice from me."

"He really is good on the stand, and I'll tell you that rude streak comes in handy in front of a jury. He's so gruff, so to the point, he seems to overshadow any other testimony. Believe me, ask him the right questions, let him answer the way he wants to and your jury won't remember any testimony but his."

"I just get the feeling he thinks I'm incompetent or something. It's not like I've never tried a case before. I've been trying murder cases for two years and I've only lost one. Granted I've only been here in Albuquerque for a few weeks, but I did come with some pretty stellar recommendations *and* I graduated Berkeley Law in the top ten percent of my class. Geez, he infuriates me."

"So it seems. Sometimes people just get off on the wrong foot, or sometimes there's a personality conflict. Or..." Sam trailed off grinning, she finished her glass of wine.

Amy frowned. "Or what?"

"Or maybe they're just attracted to the other person and too stubborn to admit it."

"Or maybe they just can't stand each other," Amy retorted.

~ * ~

As soon as he walked into his office, Zach noticed Amy waiting for him. He looked from her to Ellen and back, shook his head, and went to his desk. She followed him just as he knew she would. *What was wrong with this woman?* She was overbearing, intrusive, and much too beautiful for his taste. Not that he couldn't appreciate a beautiful woman—after all, he'd been married to one, but this one bothered him. Something about her just didn't sit right with his cop-sense. That may have made some people laugh, but he'd been at this job long enough to know that feeling when he was around people. He experienced it when he interrogated suspects, and knew the ones who were lying to him, knew the ones who told the truth.

He got certain feelings when he surveyed crime scenes—not psychic visions or anything, he didn't believe in that. But even though he couldn't put a name to what he felt when he was at a crime scene, it was never wrong. He had those same types of feelings whenever he looked at Amy Logan. Something about her just didn't sit right with him. She bothered him. And he wasn't sure if it was in a good way.

Sitting at his desk, he didn't invite her to take a seat, but she did anyway. Wearing a deep blue suit, the blazer open with a cream colored silk blouse beneath, she was conservative with the number of buttons she'd left undone. Her skirt fell at her knees, and Zach was a man who appreciated a great pair of legs. His mouth watered as he thought of kissing her. He rubbed his face with his hands, and forced himself to bring his eyes back up to her face. *Where had that come from?* He looked at her again and took the coffee Ellen brought in.

"Donut?" He gestured to the paper plate on his desk.

"No, thank you," she declined though she did accept a cup of coffee from Ellen, and then smiled her thanks at the departing secretary.

Zach frowned at her pleasantness toward Ellen when she seemed so tart toward him. What the was it about this woman that got so far under his skin? "I have work to do, Ms. Logan, so can we get to it?"

"Very well... Detective Ellison," Amy said as she lifted her briefcase, and dug around in it unnecessarily for the dramatic pause. She almost corrected the way he'd addressed her, then decided against it, knowing he'd done it to tick her off.

Then she withdrew the case file slowly, set the bag back on the floor, and thumbed through the pages as if she was looking for something in particular. Hearing his impatient sigh, she fought the smile she felt curving her lips by sticking a pen in her mouth, and tried to look thoughtful.

Though she knew the contents of the file by heart, had no need to peruse it, she was simply enjoying the irritation she was causing the man behind the desk.

He's just too good looking for his own good, Amy thought as she chewed the end of the pen. He never wore an actual suit, always jeans and a shirt with a blazer thrown over it, and his cowboy boots had little metal coverings on the toes, and he looked like one lick away from sin. A lick she thought she wouldn't mind taking... if pigs flew and there was a nuclear blast and life as it was known ceased to exist and he was the last man on earth, that is. The sound of him clearing his throat brought her back to the task at hand.

Looking up slowly from the file, she met his glare with a cool gaze. "The Louisa Gonzales murder trial starts on Wednesday, and I'm the one who got the case, so that means we have to work together. I will try to make this quick and painless... for both of us. So let's just go over some of the details so I can get an idea of what you plan on saying. You know the drill."

"The only thing I'm going to say is the facts as I know them," he said and drank his coffee.

"Which are?"

"Which are right there in your little file, I'm sure," he told her as he licked icing from his thumb.

Amy had a momentary lapse of reason and could mentally see his tongue licking certain areas of her body. Jolting when she caught the way he was looking at her, she realized she was running her tongue over her lips. He grinned broadly and licked his thumb again. He knew what she'd been thinking! And Amy felt her cheeks flush.

"I know what is in the file," she said a little more curtly than necessary. "It's what you have to say that I want to hear. And I have to be in court in a little over an hour, so if we could get this over with, I'd appreciate it." She tried to sound weary of him.

He grinned at her again and she wished he wouldn't. That curve of his lips was a dangerous weapon and she was sure he knew it as well. Busying herself with a pad of paper so she could take notes, she heard him exhale, and fought back another satisfied, if not wicked, grin.

"I received the call around ten-thirty on the night of November second of last year, and arrived at the scene some twenty minutes later. Upon arrival I saw the nude body of a Hispanic female who appeared to be in her early twenties. Upon identification of the body, it was learned she was actually nineteen. She'd been beaten and kicked to death. CSU processed the scene and the body was transported to the morgue."

"How were you able to identify the body?"

"We ran her prints through AFIS and got a hit out of L.A., where she'd been arrested on numerous occasions for prostitution and petty theft going back to a juvenile record. L.A. County P.D. found her mother and confirmed the I.D. with a photo. Her name was Louisa Gonzales and had been a misery to her mother for years. She started running away when she was twelve, got involved with drugs, began shoplifting, prostituting, and wound up dead in the desert north of I-40 near Petroglyph. Pretty simple."

"You sound real sorry for her."

"I'm not paid to feel sorry for anyone. In fact, I'm not paid to *feel,* and in this job, it's a good thing. Look, she was young and didn't have the chance to straighten out her life, but the fact remains it happens every day. That kind of life rarely turns out well. She made her choices and suffered the consequences. That may sound harsh to you, but the fact remains, it's life.

"I did my job, found the killer, who just happened to be her boyfriend, not a john like some had thought. It was too personal. He beat her too badly, kicked her even after she was dead. That was rage. A john may have beaten her if she had ripped him off, or even for the fun of it, but once she stopped fighting back he would've stopped and left her there. This one just kept beating her long after she quit fighting back. That's personal. That's love, baby."

Amy said nothing for a long moment. "Sometimes life is too much. You don't know what you'll do to survive, Ellison, because not everyone is raised like the Brady Bunch."

"Look, I'm not saying she got what she deserved—no one deserves to die like that—but you can't take it personally or it'll eat you alive. Just do your job and I'll do mine and that piece of crap in lock-up will go to prison for the rest of his life." He could see he'd hit a nerve, and what had been anger in her eyes now looked like something close to fear, and made him wonder even more about who Ms. Logan really was.

She looked at him, glanced at the clock on

the wall, and then said, "I've got to get to court. I'll see you Wednesday morning."

"Amy," he said in a softer voice as she reached for the door handle.

His voice was like a warm caress and sent shivers up her spine. "Yes?" She swallowed hard before she looked at him.

"You'll need a tougher skin if you're going to keep doing this job."

Pulling the door open, she walked out without a reply.

~ Three ~

Amy sat at the table in the front of the courtroom with two others from the District Attorney's office. Chad Johnson had just passed the bar and had been on the team for two months. Rick Sanchez had been with the District Attorney's Office for six years and was making plans to open his own office and go into criminal defense. Amy didn't mind the fact that they were there, even though this was a fairly easy case to prosecute. Chad needed the exposure, and Rick's experience was always helpful. He was a good lawyer and she knew he'd do a fine job as a defense attorney. She nearly smiled as she thought of what it might be like to be his opposing counsel one day.

The judge entered the courtroom, everyone stood as the session was called to order and the case was called. The defense made a brief opening statement. Amy followed suit, being careful to look each of the female jurors directly in the eye. There were eight women on the jury and although she liked female juries, in cases like this, it didn't always mean she had an advantage.

Juries were fickle creatures. They based decisions on emotion more than on the facts, no matter what they said. She also knew women would likely judge another woman more harshly than a man would, and wouldn't feel the sympathy for Louisa Gonzales the same way a man would. But that was the part of her job she liked. The challenge Amy Logan enjoyed was making a jury see even the vilest person as a human being with redeemable qualities though it wasn't always easy. There weren't as many loveable murder victims as one might think.

Everyone knew about the abducted and murdered child, or co-ed, or the mother of three killed by her own husband. Those types of crimes made headlines and were much easier to garner a conviction. The murdered thieves, the drug dealers, the homeless, and the prostitutes, those were the ones that made life more difficult for a prosecutor. Juries didn't feel as much sympathy for those who were criminals, or cost them more in taxes each year, and they often viewed the perpetrators as doing society a favor. But Amy didn't mind, it was part of the thrill of being a prosecutor.

She enjoyed the battle, enjoyed the tactics, and she enjoyed the moment when she saw the shift in the jury, when she knew she had them. In the five years she'd been a prosecutor, she'd lost only one case and it still haunted her. She sighed as she thought about it. She'd won countless trials, sent murderers to life sentences and to the death chamber, but no matter how many she won, it was the one she lost that haunted her dreams.

Amy had known the man was guilty. Everyone had known the man was guilty, but the jury acquitted him and Amy had never forgiven herself for not building a better case, even though no one else saw it as being her fault. The man had killed his wife and fourteen-year-old stepdaughter. He'd shot them both in his own home and had collected over a million dollars in life insurance. But he'd had an alibi... his girlfriend.

The woman had sworn he was with her all night
long and even though there was circumstantial
evidence to prove he had committed the
murders, the jury just didn't want to believe he
killed a woman and her child.

Amy could see why. She was always able to
see cases from both sides, and as much as she
wanted a conviction, she knew why she didn't
get one. The man was unfaithful, yes, but it
didn't make him a killer. And everything else
about him made him appear to be a nice guy and
the jury bought it. He had admitted to the
adultery but he'd been married to his wife for
over twelve years before he'd started an affair
with the younger woman. He had gone to a
marriage counselor and had done everything he
could to save his marriage before the affair had
started, but it just wasn't going to work. It didn't
help Amy's case that the wife had been well
aware of the affair and hadn't objected. And the
fact the wife had also taken a lover of her own
didn't help Amy make her seem like an innocent
victim.

In the end even Amy herself could almost
believe he was innocent. *Almost...* The gun was
his, he'd bought the bullets, he had planned it
down to the last detail and she knew he did it.
The worst part was he knew she knew and he just
grinned at her with a charming, boyish smile
when the verdict came back. And when he walked away from the courthouse a millionaire with a
hot little blonde on his arm, he'd grinned at Amy
and told her thanks as he walked by.

Amy shook the memory away and called
the medical examiner to the stand. Pete Strat-

ford's testimony was straightforward, technical, boring. She used the post-mortem photos he'd taken at the scene for visual affect. She got the jury reaction she wanted, and then she called the first officers from the scene, then the lead officer from the crime scene unit. She called Zach Ellison last.

"Please state your name for the record," she said after he'd been sworn in.

"Detective Zachariah Ellison," he replied, his clear voice carrying across the room.

"Please state your position with the police department, Detective."

"I'm the senior homicide detective for the northern district of New Mexico."

"How long have you held that position?"

"I've been a cop for twenty years, fifteen of it in homicide, and I've been senior detective for the northern district for the past five years."

"Thank you, Detective. Now as to the murder of Louisa Gonzales, could you tell the Court what happened that night from the time you received the call indicating a body had been found?"

He cleared his throat, turned toward the jury, and looked at each person individually. Amy glanced at the twelve men and women, noticed the men leaning forward in their seats, noticed the women noticing Zach. The younger ones' cheeks flushed when he directed his gaze at them, and the older ones smiled openly at him. By the time Zach had finished his narrative Amy could have kissed him. And so would every woman on the jury if they'd been allowed to. Maybe even some of the men, too. Zach was the kind of man who could make a woman swoon, but he was also the kind of man other men liked. The kind of man other men aspired to be, though Zach would have laughed if anyone had told him. He was very down to earth, not the least bit pretentious or self-absorbed. He was what Amy's dad would have called a regular guy. A good ol' boy who was both liked and trusted.

Amy was so giddy she thought she'd hardly even have to use her summation. She had the case, knew she had it in each of their faces. She'd known it before Zach Ellison had stepped out of the witness box after his cross examination by the defense. And she'd seen it in the other lawyer's face as well. Looking over at the defense table, she saw the defendant was staring at the table while his attorney whispered in his ear. She didn't know exactly what Conroy might be telling his client, but Amy knew if it was the other way around, she'd be trying to talk the prosecutor into rethinking the deal they'd turned down earlier. But she tried not to look overly confidant as she thanked the witness and rested her case.

The judge called a recess for lunch and Amy caught Zach in the hallway. "I want to apologize to you, Zach," she said. "And I want to thank you."

He held up his hand. "Don't worry about it. I should be apologizing to you as well. I think we just got off on the wrong foot. Truce?" He held out his hand.

She smiled and hesitated, then put her hand in his. She wasn't prepared for the electricity that seemed to sizzle at the contact and shoot straight up her arm. She withdrew her hand, looked at it, and then looked into his eyes. He grinned that lopsided grin of his, turned on his heel and walked away. She stared stupidly at her hand and then at him as he made his way down the corridor.

"Ms. Logan?"

The voice startled her out of her stupor. "Yes?" She turned to face the other attorney. "Mr. Conroy, what can I do for you?" She smiled pleasantly.

"Is that plea offer still on the table?"

She took a breath. "Mr. Conroy, you and I both know I have a conviction here. You have nothing to bargain with."

"Take the death penalty off, we'll plead guilty, and agree to life without parole. He thought he could beat it, like they all do." Conroy shrugged with a small smile. "So the twenty-five to life you'd offered seemed too excessive to him even in the face of death. But he's sweating it now and a life sentence is looking pretty good."

Cocking her head to one side, she looked at him. "I'm feeling generous today, Mr. Conroy. Tell your boy he's got a deal."

After lunch, court reconvened and the judge was informed of the plea agreement. The jury was thanked for their time and the case was closed. Amy began putting her files away, the records back into their boxes. "Thanks for your help, Chad," she told the young lawyer.

"I didn't do anything." He smiled at her.

"You helped with research, you were here. We're a team, Chad, it all helps."

"You're welcome," he said and beamed at her before taking the boxes from her and carrying them out of the courthouse.

"He'll be sniffing at your heels from now on," Rick said with a laugh.

Amy smiled back. "He's just eager to learn and he's easy to work with, so I won't mind."

"How about dinner tonight?"

"Rick, you know I don't date people I work with," she told him.

"It's not a date, Amy. I want to talk business with you over dinner. I have a proposition for you." His dimples showed in both cheeks.

She recognized the teasing in his voice. "I don't proposition with those I work with either," she teased back.

He laughed. "Okay, a business dinner, that's all."

"Okay. I should be done around six today, how about you?"

He looked at his watch and calculated. "Hmmm, probably a little later than that, so how about meeting me at Guadalupe's around eight?"

"Great, it'll give me time to go home and change, get out of these heels."

"See you then," he said, picking up the last box to carry out with him.

~ * ~

Amy was the first to arrive at Guadalupe's just before eight, so settled into a table and ordered a Margarita. She had changed out of her suit into jeans and a tank top that left little of her breasts unexposed. Her hair was tied back into a ponytail and she wore flip-flops on her feet. She resembled the co-eds from the university more than she did an attorney. Sucking on the straw in her drink, she plucked the lime off the rim and bit into it, puckering as she did.

~ * ~

That was the scene Zach saw when he walked into the restaurant with Ron Petrie. Zach told his companion to go ahead and get a table, saying he'd be right back and then he walked slowly toward Amy's table. He drank in the sight of her, and let her fill his senses. She was beautiful and she took his breath away. She had since the first time he'd laid eyes on her, but it had been so long since he'd felt anything even close to physical attraction to a woman, he hadn't even recognized it. He sure recognized it now.

Not that he wanted to do anything about it, not yet at least. But he didn't think anything was wrong with keeping the feeling humming through his blood stream for a little while longer.

"Eating alone?"

Amy's head jerked up at the sound of his voice and her eyes went wide. "Zach. What are you doing here?"

"Didn't mean to startle you." He grinned.

"Oh," she fumbled. "You didn't. I'm waiting for someone."

"Hmm," was all he could think of to say. He had gotten an eyeful of her and now he was embarrassed. He dragged his gaze from her body to a point on the wall across the room, and took a deep breath to steady himself.

"Amy, sorry I'm late," a male voice said from behind Zach. "Detective, good to see you. Rick Sanchez," the man introduced himself, offering his hand as Zach turned around.

"Rick," Zach said and shook his hand. "How's it going?" He looked at Amy and said, "Have a nice evening. Both of you."

~ * ~

"You and the detective getting to be pretty chummy, huh?" Rick commented as he slid into the booth.

Amy laughed. "Hardly. We can barely be in the same room together without fighting. He just rubs me the wrong way."

"What looks good tonight?"

"I'm thinking enchiladas or the chili rellenos," she said and looked over the menu. She ordered another Margarita when the waitress brought a bowl of tortilla chips and fresh salsa.

"I'll have a Tecate," Rick told the waitress, "and the combination plate sounds good."

The waitress looked expectantly at Amy, who said, "I don't know, the chili rellenos, I guess." Amy handed the girl the menu and she walked away.

"So," Amy said, dipping a chip in the salsa, "what's this business you want to discuss?"

"No small talk, huh?" He reached for a chip, his eyes grazing over Amy.

She finished the first Margarita, and pushed the empty glass to the middle of the table. "Sorry, I just like getting things over with." The waitress brought the fresh drinks and set them on the table.

Rick squeezed a lime into the opening of the longneck bottle, then pushed it into the liquid and took a long pull off the Mexican beer.

"You know I've given notice downtown. I've got ten days left and then I'm going solo."

"So I've heard." She chuckled. "Cooper almost had a stroke."

Rick laughed and took another pull from the bottle of beer. "You should've seen it from my point of view. Every vein in his neck was bulging, and the big one on his forehead was pulsating. I thought he'd stroke out right there." They both laughed.

"I so hope he doesn't get elected next fall."

Rick chuckled, "I'm not voting for him."

They clinked their drinks together, and Amy laughed. "Me either."

The waitress brought their plates, set them on the table, picked up the empty beer bottle and gestured toward Rick. He nodded and she hurried off to get him another.

"I'm going to be in private practice for the first time in my life, and I'm excited about it. I was hoping you'd want to form a partnership, work with me. You're one of the best lawyers I know."

She forked a bit of rice into her mouth and swallowed. "Thanks, but I'm a prosecutor."

"And a darn fine one, but don't you ever think about the other side, defending the indefensible, fighting for the underdog?"

Looking at him, she replied, "Of course, but a dead nineteen-year-old hooker *is* the underdog. That's who I was fighting for this morning."

He poked at his meal, finally took a bite of the enchilada. "I know you were."

They ate in silence for several minutes, then he asked, "Did you hear about that case in Phoenix a couple of years back? The dad who went to prison for shooting the man who molested his daughter?"

"Yeah, I was working in L.A. when that happened. It ticked me off."

"Ticked off everyone, but I bring it up because I want to know where you would've wanted to be when that case came to trial?"

"I can't answer that," she said, stirred her drink and swallowed the remainder. "Yes, I can. I would have still wanted to be in the D.A.'s office so I could've made some heads roll for even thinking of prosecuting. They should've given him a medal."

Rick laughed. "They should've, but the system failed in that case and the dad got more time than the child molester did. But that's a case I would have loved to defend. You haven't eaten much, aren't you hungry?"

"Not really, but it was good."

"I'll have the waitress wrap it for you. You can take it home. Eat it in the morning."

"I won't eat it, so why don't you take it?"

"Okay, I will. A minute in the microwave and it'll be a nice, hot breakfast. Want another drink?"

"No thanks. Two is my limit. I have to be up early in the morning. I'll think about your offer, though. Thanks for dinner," she said, sliding out of the booth and heading for the door.

Rick watched her go, took a deep breath and finished his beer. She was as fine as wine and he has hoping for a little taste. Maybe after he went into his own practice he'd ask her out on a real date, since she didn't date in the office and he wouldn't be in the office then. He walked outside and lit a cigarette, inhaled deeply. He'd been jonesin' for one all night but knew Amy didn't smoke, so he'd refrained. Blowing the smoke out in a great puff, he walked to his car.

~ * ~

Zach watched Amy as she left the restaurant, considered intercepting her, and then decided against it. He'd been stealing sideways glances at her all evening, and had seen her laughing at something Rick said. He didn't know why, but it irritated him.

Crap. The beer in his hand was getting warm. He ate the last of the meal in front of him, scooted his plate back and watched Rick leave. Zach didn't know he was going to follow Amy until he was already standing.

"See ya tomorrow, Ron. I gotta get home."

Ron stood and said, "Me, too. Leslie will be waiting up for me and if she finds out we've been out to dinner without her, she'll shoot both of us. I told her we were just going to stop off for a beer."

"Well, that does it, you're a dead man. I'll work the case myself," Zach said with a wry grin.

"Thanks," Ron said dryly.

Zach tossed some bills onto the table and strolled into the night air. Climbing into his Avalanche, he started the vehicle and merged with the other traffic. He knew where Amy lived. Not that it was important for him to know, he just liked staying on top of things with the people he worked with. He wasn't going to visit her, he told himself, and he definitely wasn't spying on her, he just wanted to swing by to make sure she was safe. It was *just* a welfare check. He was a cop after all.

Turning down the narrow street, making his way slowly, looking at the numbers on the houses, he found 3407 and saw her little blue car in the driveway. He came to a stop in front of her house, saw a light burning in the window but saw no movement. Relieved that Rick's car wasn't there, he still waited a few minutes, and watched until the light went out before he drove away.

~ * ~

Amy heard an engine idling in front of her house and peeked through a crack in the curtain. It looked like Zach Ellison's SUV to her.

Now what does he think he's doing in front of my house?

Not knowing why he'd be spying on her, or following her, she didn't like it one bit and would make a point about it in the morning. Then she turned off the lights and went to bed. She shut her eyes but Zach's face filled her mind.

"Oh, go away," she muttered.

~ Four ~

It had been over a week since she'd had the nightmares. She'd had them most of her life, since early childhood really, and remembered waking up so scared she couldn't even get out of bed to go to the bathroom. They'd continued, worsened as she grew older, but now it had been more than a week and she didn't remember the last time she'd actually slept all night long, or the last time she felt this good. Walking into the bathroom, she turn-ed the taps in the shower and stepped under the hot spray. She let it run over her head and beat against her neck and shoulders, with her eyes closed.

The face appeared in her mind's eye, the way it had looked right before he'd died, and it brought a smile to her lips. Her face had been the last thing he'd seen before she had sent him to hell.

Hmmm, she thought, *that was when the nightmares had stopped*. Had she finally put her demons to rest by taking his life? It seemed much more than a coincidence to her but even if it wasn't, it was nice to finally have slept through the night, to feel this rested just once.

She shampooed her hair, leaned back and let the spray rinse the lather down her back, and then she worked conditioner through it, soaped her body, and used the loofa. After shaving her legs, she turned off the taps, and wrapped a towel around her head and one around her body and went back into the bedroom to dress.

She didn't know when it had occurred to her to actually kill him. She'd thought about killing him, and the others, for so many years but that was during the anger, the hurt, the humiliation of it all. She'd often thought of just buying a gun, finding them all and starting shooting. She'd imagined them dying in fiery crashes, being hit by a bus, drowning in their bathtubs, overdosing on drugs, falling and breaking their necks—any way at all, by fair means or foul. As long as they died, she would've been happy.

But that was when she had cried, when the pain was so raw she could hardly function, barely make it through a day. And the nights, forget the nights. She went days with no sleep, and had turned to drugs, to alcohol, to other men, anything and anyone to help ease the torture in her soul. But nothing had.

Years had gone by. She got older and maybe she just finally grew up and came to accept that she couldn't change the past, only learn to live with it. Pain became distant, and eventually she could think of the atrocities perpetrated upon her without feeling the gut-wrenching pain that had been there before. It became distant. Past. Done. Over with. It was nothing that affected her life anymore. At least she didn't think it really affected her life anymore.

That was when she changed her life. Became another person, went to college, and received a degree in psychology. It was therapy. She'd broken down and cried in a lot of the classes she took because the things she studied brought it all back to her. And she discovered she really hadn't dealt with her past after all. But after spending four years getting her degree, she finally understood her life then, the craziness of it all, and for the first time in her life, she felt normal. She felt like she had some bit of control over her own life. But she hadn't found complete peace because the nightmares still came, and sometimes she'd find herself awake at three in the morning, watching old movies on TV, drinking coffee, and smoking cigarettes.

That was when she'd started planning to kill them. It hadn't been a conscious thought at all, not something she'd sat down and decided to do. It had just happened in the subtlest of ways. While watching a mystery on TV, when the murder had been committed, she'd find herself thinking she could do *that* to one of them. And then she found herself daydreaming about it at the oddest times.

Years passed but the thought of exacting revenge didn't. And the surprise was that she didn't even feel hurt, or anger, or betrayal, or any of those things she'd felt in the past. There were no hot feelings toward anyone anymore, just cold, calculated longing to see them die at her own hand. To make sure the last thing they saw before they went to hell was her face, so they'd remember why they were dispatched there in the first place. So they'd see her face before them for all of eternity.

She had always wanted to start in order, the first offender to be punished first, and so on down the line until she'd killed them all. But that didn't happen. Her father's oldest brother had died of cancer years and years ago. He would have been the first. She was three the first time he'd touched her, and he'd told her if she told her daddy, he would tell her daddy she was lying, and she knew what her daddy would do if she lied to him. She knew. She also knew her daddy would believe his brother before he believed her. It went on until she was nearly eleven years old.

Every time they went to visit her uncle and his family, he'd find a way to get her into his workshop and lock her in with him. Sitting her up on the work bench, he would take her clothes off and fondle her, telling her he would make her a woman, would teach her things she'd never learn anywhere else. She remembered one particular trip when she was five or six when he kept trying to penetrate her with his penis, and it simply wasn't going to happen, but he kept pressing her, and she cried because it hurt. He told her to shut up because someone would hear if she cried, and he told her it would stop hurting once the head was in, but it just wouldn't go in. Then he got mad because she cried harder, so he stopped. Just about then, her sister and cousin came beating on the shop door wanting to know why they couldn't come in too.

Oh, how she wanted to kill him, but not outright. Slowly. So slowly, so painfully, until he cried out and begged her to stop. But no, he got lung cancer and died. But, he did die slowly and that was some comfort. The doctors cut one piece of his lung away at a time until he had barely half a lung left. He was on a morphine drip for the pain, but it never really went away no matter how much morphine he had, and the last months of his life were excruciating. Maybe that was justice after all. Maybe the pain followed him to hell as well. Maybe God had sorted it out for her.

The second one was her mother's youngest brother. He'd molested her too. It had started when she was about seven, while it was still going on with the other uncle, but her mother's brother never tried to actually have sex with her; he just wanted her to touch him. Somehow, in her young, messed up mind, it seemed better than what the other uncle was doing to her. It seemed less offensive because at least he wasn't hurting her. So she would stroke his penis when he told her to, would kiss it when he told her to, and never said a word to anyone, just like he told her to. He died of cancer as well. He'd been in Vietnam, exposed to Agent Orange, and died a slow, painful death. It seemed fair. Well, it seemed almost fair. If he couldn't die at her hand, then she'd have to be satisfied his death came slowly and painfully.

She hadn't even intended to kill Clarence Broom, at least not when it had happened. After all, she'd just been thinking about it, going through it in her head. It helped, but she never saw herself *actually* doing it. Never thought she would do it, but had no doubt she was capable if the circumstance ever presented itself. Then she'd gone to California on a little vacation to get out of the blasted heat of the desert. She really didn't like living there but a good paying job had presented itself, so she'd made the move. She had quit her psychology practice— she'd just gotten tired of it, of her clients, of hearing the same story over and over, until she just wanted to slap their whining mouths. There was too much of her own past in them, so she just quit. Having always dreamed of being a lawyer, she went back to school, got her degree, landed the job in Albuquerque, New Mexico, and there she was.

She had driven to California. She did love to drive through the desert at night—Lord knew you couldn't drive through it during the day with temperatures reaching well over a hundred degrees. At night at least it dropped down to the low nineties. But there were stars in the desert, millions and millions of stars, and she'd stopped alongside the road and lay on the hood of her car and just stared at them. That was the closest feeling to peace, the closest feeling to God she'd ever known.

Driving through the Mojave Desert, she went through the town of Tehachapi, down the mountain into the valley of Bakersfield and out to Interstate 5, which ran the length of California and on into Oregon and Washington. She'd been born and raised in northern California where the mountains fell into the ocean, and she missed it but knew she'd never go back except to visit. She drove on northward to the city of Redding, took Highway 299 west through the Trinity Alps to the little town of Weaverville where she had been raised—or at least it was the only place that had felt like home.

Spending three days in the mountains, tripping around the Trinity River, lying in the warm summer sun was just what she needed but she had a job to get back to, and that's when it had happened. She had driven back through the winding mountain roads and headed south on Interstate 5, then she continued on to Highway

58 into Bakersfield, where she stopped for the night. Rising early the next morning, she left the motel, and stopped at a convenience store for coffee and gas, and then she saw him.

It had been so many years, she wasn't even really sure it was him. He was on the sidewalk, sticking out his thumb trying to hitch a ride. Quickly concluding her business, she got into her car, and pulled slowly out onto the street. She recognized him, older, but definitely him. Pulling up beside him, she asked if he needed a ride, so he hopped in and hadn't even recognized her. He said he was headed out to Taft, the small town where he worked and she said that was where she was going too, and just like that she had him.

As she took the road to Taft she thought of what she could do with him, how she could possibly get him back to New Mexico. He sounded like the same cocky jackass she'd remembered him as, and he was hitting on her unashamedly. Turning toward him, she smiled sweetly, and as easy as that, he agreed to go with her. Of course, he had wanted money, but she had cash now, and she gave him half up front.

When they finally arrived in Albuquerque it was early morning and she was exhausted. Showing him to a room he could use, she simply waited for him to go to sleep. When she heard him snoring, she'd gone quietly to the room and shook him. There was no response. Obviously a deep sleeper, she tied him to the bed, and then she went to sleep. Hours later she heard him shouting at the top of his lungs, so she pulled herself out of bed to shut him up. Cursing at the top of his lungs, he was making threats and promises simultaneously, so she shoved a roll of socks in his mouth and tied them in place behind his head, then went back to bed.

When she woke up it was early evening. She showered, fixed some coffee and a bit of breakfast, then went to check on him. He was awake, his eyes wide. She asked if he needed to pee and he nodded, so she took the bottle she carried in her hand to the bed, unzipped his pants and held it in a way he could relieve himself. It took him a minute, but he finally peed, and she took care of the contents, went back in the bedroom and shoved a handful of sleeping pills down his throat, forcing him to swallow, and then left him alone.

It was after midnight when she went back into the bedroom, he was still sleeping, but she poked him, shook him, and twisted the shorthairs on the back of his neck just to make sure he wasn't faking it. His eyes had fluttered and she could see the glazed look in them telling her he wasn't ready to wake yet, so she untied him. Then she pulled him to a sitting position and got him to his feet. He wasn't much taller than she was, but he was heavier and took all her strength to keep him from falling as she half-carried and half led him through the kitchen to the garage door and tossed him in the back-seat of her car. Pulling his hands behind his back, she used zip ties to handcuff him and bind his ankles together, and then she threw a blanket over him. The trunk of her car had everything she'd need already packed in it, so all she had to do was find the perfect spot to do it.

She drove out into the desert, a place she'd remembered from when she first arrived in New Mexico, and had gone exploring the area, familiarizing herself with her surroundings. The area was to the east of the city in the mountains, though the trees were sparse, it was beautiful. Taking the two-lane paved road to her left, she continued driving until she came to a one-lane dirt road that turned left, then curved right, going deep into the mountains. There weren't any homes, or other signs of human life for miles as she finally came to the spot she'd been looking for. The moon was full and washed the land in soft light. Once she was out of the vehicle, she opened the trunk and began preparing for the deed she was about to carry out.

Finally, when she'd prepared everything, she pulled him out of the car. He was awake and trying to fight her, trying to yell through the gag on his mouth, so she pulled the pistol out of her pocket and laid it against his forehead, and he knew she meant business.

"If you try to fight I will have no problem killing you right now."

She used a knife to cut the ties at his ankles, stripped his jeans and underwear from him, and then made him walk to the trees barefoot. There were two smaller ones about six or seven feet apart with no low branches, and she made him sit at the base of one and tied his ankle to it with the nylon rope she'd brought, then tied the other foot to the other tree.

She pulled him to his feet, checked the ropes, tied another piece of rope to one wrist before she cut the zip ties off of him, and then tied one hand to one tree, the other hand to the other tree, just like she had with his feet. After he was secure, she retrieved a folding step stool, opened it and climbed up on it.

"I'm going to untie one wrist, but if you try anything, I'll taze you," she said, producing the taser from her pocket.

Untying one wrist, she was now able to pull it higher on the tree, and then adjusted the other one in the same manner so he was spread eagle between them. His hands were purple from the lack of circulation, but that was of no concern while she used the knife to cut his shirt off him so he was nude before her.

That's when she started talking to him, telling him all about himself, but he still didn't know who she was. *Had she really ever been afraid of this sniveling, whining pig?* She laughed at him then, told him who she was and saw his eyes go wide. Taking the gag from his mouth, she dribbled a little water over his tongue so he could talk, and all he could manage was to cuss her, so she hit him with the stun gun. When he'd recovered, she told him he would get more of the same if he didn't behave, and when he cursed her, she hit him with the electrical charge again. He hadn't changed at all... he was still the same creep he'd always been. He was threatening her, just like he used to do. He began telling her how he'd kill her, how his friends would find her and kill her for him. She laughed out loud then. She was no longer afraid of him. *She* had the upper hand this time, and she couldn't believe the sense of power it gave her. She hit him with the stun gun one more time just because she could and then she laughed.

Relating everything to him then, she told him how he'd abused her when they'd lived together, how it felt being abused, beaten, handcuffed to a door and raped. Told him how it had haunted her all those years, all the fear he'd instilled in her, the nightmares she'd had because of him. How she left California because of it, how she'd never gotten over the baby he'd caused her to deliver too early for the little boy to survive. She went on and on, leaving out nothing, reminding him of every vile thing he'd ever done, of every moment he'd terrorized her. Even after he'd gone to prison for rape, he'd continued to terrorize her from behind prison walls.

Then she grabbed his limp, little male part with one hand, gripped it tightly, and slid the edge of a knife over his stomach. She shaved a patch of pubic hair as she made the trail to the base of his penis where it was attached to his body. He started to beg then. Oh, how she'd delighted in hearing him beg. But she didn't cut him, no, instead she yanked. She pulled as hard as she could with her hand fisted tightly around his penis, and heard him scream as the skin peeled right off. It was just like peeling the casing off a sausage. Looking at the flaccid skin in her hand—at the horror and pain contorting his face, she just grinned. Then she sliced his it off as close to his stomach as she could. He bellowed then, screamed like a two-year-old girl, and she shoved it as deep in his throat as she could, until the gagging stopped.

Opening the little bag she had with her, she pulled out a leather strip about an inch wide, soaked it in the jug of water she'd brought, and tied it tightly around his throat. Then she took the rest of the water and poured it over him, washing him as she went, ridding his body of any trace evidence he might have picked up while at her house or in her car. She had no intention of going to prison for the likes of him. She cleaned the area of everything, put it back in the trunk of her car, left the rubber gloves on her hands, and went back to him.

Grabbing him by the hair of the head, she pulled his face forward so he had to look her in the eyes, then she told him she wanted her face to be the last thing he saw before he went to hell, and the first he saw when he woke up there. Sliding the knife into the soft flesh just above the pubic bone, she drew it all the way up his stomach in a slow, straight line to the sternum. She could hear odd, strangled sounds in his throat as his entrails spilled onto the ground between his legs.

Then she stepped back and watched the light in his eyes fade as he died. Looking up at the full moon, then back at the dead body before her, she thought, *Blood really did appear quite black in moon light.*

Pausing for a moment as she considered what she'd just seen, she looked at his dead, open eyes. She'd seen the life fade from them. She hadn't realized it was like that when someone died. Taking a deep breath, she blew it out and set about cleaning up the mess, then peeled the gloves from her hands, dropped them in the plastic garbage bag, and used the remaining water to wash the blood from her feet and legs.

Then she stepped into a pair of flip-flops, picked up the bag and jug, walked back to her car and drove home.

It was not yet light out when she pulled into the garage. She let the door slide down behind her, stripped out of her tank top and shorts and put them in the bag along with the towel she'd used to cover the front seat of her car where she had sat. Then she put the blanket in the washing machine and turned the knobs, went into the house, took a shower and dressed. Afterwards, she put the tools she'd used away, took the garbage bag out back, put it in the burn barrel, doused it with gasoline and dropped a match to it.

Back inside, she stripped the bed where he'd been, vacuumed the mattress and floor, dusted the furnishings, and remade the bed. Satisfied at last that the room was clean, she went into the living room and lay down on the couch. Feeling nothing but exhaustion, she fell asleep. The distant sound of the alarm clock woke her, and she saw the clock on the wall, it was 5:30 a.m. and she still had a job to get to.

Fixing a pot of coffee, she dressed while it brewed, poured it into her travel mug and backed her car out of the garage. Stopping at the car wash on her way, she drove through the automated side, stopped by the vacuum and cleaned the inside, and then the trunk. Now that she was satisfied that there'd be no evidence to link her to his body, she drove to work with a satisfied smile on her lips.

~ Five ~

"Good morning, Zach." Amy didn't wait to be invited in as she walked into his office.

He looked up from his paper work and sighed. "What can I do for you, Amy?"

"What were you doing on the street in front of my house last night?" she demanded as she shut the door behind her.

He leaned back in his chair, and looked her up and down without trying to hide it. She didn't shift or flinch but continued to level a gaze at him. He leaned forward and grinned at her. "My job."

"Your job? How is being in front of my house at night your job?"

"I don't like the guy, okay? I just wanted to make sure he didn't follow you home is all," he said with a shrug.

"Perhaps I wanted him to follow me home, and even if I didn't, it's none of your business. I am a grown woman and I decide who comes into my home. *Not* you. I don't want your protection, don't need your protection, and if I did need protection, you're not the one I'd ask. Got it? Good." She whirled around, jerked open the door and left his office without shutting it. He grinned after her and didn't mind the door standing open.

She's feisty and determined and the woman sends fire through my veins. Zach exhaled deeply.

It had been so long since he'd had feelings like that, he wasn't sure what he wanted to do about it. If he was a different person, he'd just go with it. He'd take her out to dinner, take her home, and fill himself with the sight, scent, and sound of her. But he knew himself well enough to know he wasn't another person. Zach didn't just take carelessly.

He never had. Well, maybe in those days when he was a young man in college and hormones ran wild. He'd had more than his share of women back in the days when he was no more than a young buck with something to prove, but he'd still taken care with those he slept with. Now he wasn't a young man anymore, and he'd experienced love and devotion on the deepest of levels with Stacie. He still missed Stacie, still loved her, but it wasn't the searing ache and desperate loss he'd felt after she died. He'd come to terms with it, had dealt with it, and had gone on without her. If he hadn't dated, or hadn't slept with another woman in the years since Stacie had died, it was only because he'd yet to meet one that stirred his blood. Until now.

Leaning over the desk, he pushed thoughts of both Amy and Stacie aside, and went back to work. They had so little to go on. The killer had been very careful about not leaving any evidence behind, but the one thing Zach knew was they always made a mistake. Eventually. He had his own theory about the case, but theories didn't put anyone behind bars and it certainly didn't stand up in court. Right now he didn't know anymore about the case than he had when he'd first arrived at the murder scene, but he did have more on the victim. He couldn't imagine anyone was grieving the loss of the murdered man, but the file sure gave him a long list of potential suspects. In fact, he was surprised someone hadn't offed this guy a long time ago.

Sometimes his job made no sense to him, and it became more so the older he got, the more he saw. There were some cases, like this murder, where it seemed like justice had been served. The guy had been convicted of rape, theft, and an assortment of other petty crimes, but the things he'd never been convicted of were what interested Zach the most. He was a drug addict, fed off women with young children on welfare. He had abused the women and their children, and had left them running scared with no one to help them. The long list of complaints had never resulted in arrest as the women generally either ran or refused to testify. Zach had never understood either side of that situation.

Why a man felt the need to bully and belittle a woman or child was beyond him. And why the women stayed, why they refused to testify and put the guy away was a puzzle as well. He had heard their stories, knew the fear that had been instilled in them, the way they had been brainwashed into believing they were worthless. They'd been battered into thinking no one else would want them, bullied into believing they could never have another life, but he knew he couldn't truly understand.

He thought like a man of course, a man that had been raised to respect women, to protect them, to be gentle with them in every aspect. And as a man, he also thought men like the one who'd been strung up and murdered really got better than he deserved. He wasn't looking forward to hauling in the person who'd killed

Clarence Broom, but he would because it was his job and he did his job very well.

He read more of the file and found nothing that made him think anything other than what he'd come up with earlier. He still had that niggling in the back of his mind that made him think a woman had committed this crime. He shook his head. *Could a woman have been so ruthless?* He closed the file and called Pete.

"I need to see your notes," Zach told him.

"I sent my report up there."

"I know you did, Pete. I want your notes."

Pete blew out a breath, "Okay. You want me to send them up?"

"No, I'm on my way down. I may have questions for you," Zach said.

"Imagine that." Zach heard Pete mutter just before hanging up.

~ * ~

Zach sat on a stool near the table where Pete was performing an autopsy, reading Pete's handwritten notes. Pete always jotted down everything he thought—all of his theories, ideas, glimmers, and inklings—right along with all of the notes pertaining to the autopsy itself. What Pete said during the autopsy was recorded, but what he thought was written down later. Zach had found Pete's perceptions in the past to be very helpful and he liked what he was reading this afternoon.

Chuckling, Zach asked, "You think it was a woman?"

Pete didn't bother to look up from his work. "Uh-huh."

"It's a pretty gruesome way to commit

murder for a woman. You know most women who murder use poison. They don't like the mess murder causes."

"Uh-huh," Pete grunted and continued working.

"So you're not going to tell me why you think the murder was committed by a woman?"

"Uh-uh."

"I'm taking this with me. Call me later when you can talk." Zach rose and walked toward the door.

"Zach, she cleaned him up. It was too neat, too tidy, too *female.*"

Pausing, Zach leaned on the door jam. "It could just mean it was professional, or that he'd done it before, or maybe it means he's a cop and knows what we look for. Or maybe he's one of those obsessive/compulsive types who wash their hands fifty times a day."

"Maybe," Pete shrugged. "But I doubt it."

"Okay." Zach pushed the door open, went through and let it click shut behind him.

Back at his desk, Zach looked over Pete's notes again, this time playing devil's advocate. He had to know if he was on the right track, but now that Pete had said the very same thing Zach was thinking about this case, he knew he was right.

A woman... really?

~ * ~

Weeks went by and every lead, as few as there were, was followed up on. Pete's notes were nearly worn out from Zach reading them so much, and he'd collected a list of all the women Clarence Broom had dated, lived with, married, or had known casually. Or at least as much of a list as he could find. Every woman on it had a reason to kill Clarence and not one of them stood out more than any other. This guy had been a real piece of work. Zach was getting frustrated.

On Monday morning Zach made his way to his desk and settled in just as the door opened. "Zach." Ron stuck his head in the office. "There's another one."

Zach looked up. "Another one? Body?"

"Yep, and it sounds like the same guy as in the Broom case."

"Great," Zach said through clenched teeth as he pulled his blazer off the back of the chair and stuck his arms into the sleeves.

They drove through traffic in Zach's Avalanche, pulled onto Interstate 40 and headed west. Taking the exit that led past the big truck stop on the south side of the freeway, they continued south for several miles. They found the dirt road and followed it until they came to the foothills, and could see flashing lights for half a mile before they got there—it looked like every cop in Albuquerque was on the scene.

Zach walked through the crowd of cops and Ron pulled everyone back so Zach could make his ritual walk around the body. Zach looked the scene over for several minutes, and then, with hands behind his back, he began slowly walking around the body in a wide circle with his head tilted to one side.

Well, he thought, *no mistake this was done by the same killer as in the Broom case.*

The male body hung between two small

trees, with a leather band tied around his neck, leaving his face purplish and swollen. His penis had been severed and was now protruding from his mouth. This body however, had not been gutted like a fish, but when Zach walked around behind the body, he stopped and stared. Protruding from the anus was the handle of a Louisville Slugger. Zach shook his head. If this was the work of a woman, she had a set of *cajones* that were not only brass, but dragged the ground.

"Hey," Pete said to Zach as he ducked under the yellow crime scene tape. "This is different."

Zach glanced up. "Yeah, to say the least."

"Looks like the same perp to me," Pete commented as he began working.

Zach nodded and sighed loudly. "I'll see you back at the office. Let me know when you get there."

"No problem."

Zach left Ron in charge, ordering everyone to keep back until the medical examiner and CSU had finished their jobs, although he was sure they'd find little, if any, evidence. If it was the same person, and he was almost sure it was, the body had been washed clean. Zach climbed back into his Avalanche and drove back to the city. This time he managed to get back into his office before the press had swarmed the building.

~ * ~

"So what's the story on this one, Zach?" Amy walked into his office without knocking.

"Amy, go away," he said as he scrubbed his hands over his face, but she sat down on the chair across from his desk.

"I hear it's the same guy," she said, crossing her legs, exposing a good deal of thigh.

Zach studied the paper on his desk without looking up. "I said go away, Amy, not have a seat."

"I heard you, but I want information on this murder," she said.

She clenched her teeth and folded her hands in her lap to keep from fidgeting, hating the effect this man had on her. Those blue eyes of his seemed to look right through her and she couldn't help but wonder how all his thick, dark hair would feel sliding through her fingers, how those full lips would feel brushing across hers.

"I don't have any information, Amy. I haven't been back in my office more than five minutes. How do you seem to know everything that goes on over here anyway?"

"I have my sources, Detective. It is my job to stay on top of things, you know." She hoped she sounded as cool as she intended to.

"No, it's not your job. Your job is to prosecute criminals that have already been arrested. It's my job to investigate and bring those criminals in so you can prosecute them. Why are you so interested in this case anyway?"

"Are you kidding? This is the biggest case this city has ever seen. It's going to make my career here."

Zach nodded. She was ambitious. She was also a pain in the ass. "Fine, make your career, but stay out of my way, okay?"

"Will you call me when you know something then?"

"No. Now go away. I have work to do."

"Fine," she said as she stood and smoothed her skirt. "I'll be back." She turned and walked out the open door.

Zach took a deep breath and tapped his pencil against the pad on his desk. Didn't that woman just drive him crazy? And not just because she was the most stubborn, irritating, obstinate woman he'd ever known, but because all of those were traits he admired in a woman—along with intelligence and beauty, which she also had. His mind was filled with the thought of her in the tank top she'd been wearing that night at the restaurant a few weeks earlier. He'd never seen her dressed in anything other than her business suits until then, and now he wished he hadn't seen her in the thin white material that women only wore when they wanted to be noticed.

"Knock it off, Ellison," he admonished himself with a shake of his head. There was work to do, so he opened the case file and began writing, and worked through lunch without a break. When he finally stood to stretch, the phone on his desk rang.

"Zach, the body just arrived down here. Thought you'd want to be here for the autopsy," Pete said when Zach answered.

"On my way." He put the phone on the base, and then picked it up again. If Amy wanted information on the case, he'd just give it to her. He dialed the number from the card she'd left him, waited for the automated service, then punched in the extension.

"Amy? Zach here. The body just came in to the morgue. I'm going down—want to join me?" He looked at the phone in his hand and grinned.

Amy hadn't even bothered to hang up on her end before he'd heard the door of her office slam.

Taking the elevator down, he pushed open the double doors that led to the morgue, and entered the autopsy room where he put on a face shield and paper apron. Ron was standing by the table with Pete, already wearing the protective gear.

"What do we have here?" Zach asked, putting on latex gloves.

"Just about to start, but I have to tell you, Zach, I've never seen anything like this. This is morbid—even for me," Pete said, shaking his head.

Ron nodded. "I've been in homicide for ten years, Zach. I can't believe this one."

"Yeah, let's get on with it," Zach said and took a breath. He hated autopsies as well, but they were a vital part of finding evidence, and at this point he needed all he could get.

The doors opened again as Amy walked in, still out of breath, and all three men looked up. Zach thought she must have run the entire three blocks from her office.

"This is Amy Logan, D.A.'s office," Zach said and made introductions. "There's an apron and a face shield on the shelf," he told her and pointed. "Put them on."

She nodded and when she was wearing the protective gear, she made her way to Zach's side and stood staring wide-eyed at the body on the table.

Pete took photos of the body—the penis in the mouth, a close-up of the face, and of particular areas like the leather band around the throat. He removed the penis from the mouth, and photographed the teeth. Moving over the body, he photographed the bruises and burn marks on the upper torso, and the ligature marks on the ankles and wrists. The body was on its side because of the baseball bat protruding from the rectum, and he photographed that as well.

"Okay. I'm going to pull this out first, so I can turn the body," he said at length. "It's not going to be pretty."

Pete grasped the handle of the bat with one hand and placed a gloved hand on the corpse's hip and pulled. The bat didn't budge. He grasped the bat with both hands and twisted it to the right, then braced a hand against the hip again and pulled harder, but it still wouldn't budge.

He looked up at Zach. "Want to give me a hand here?"

Zach blew out a breath and walked around the table while pulling on a second pair of gloves. *No*, he thought, *I definitely do not want to help on this one.*

He held the body in place while Pete twisted the bat back and forth a few times and then pulled slowly. It made a loud sucking noise and when the bat finally came out, blood, water, feces, and pieces of intestines gushed out after it, splattering onto Pete and Zach both, and then splashed noisily onto the floor at their feet.

"All righty then," Pete commented, and held up the sawed off bat, glancing at Zach, and then he showed Amy and Ron.

Amy made a sound that wasn't quite a scream as she turned and ran to the sink, and heaved her lunch into it. Zach took a deep breath and shrugged as he looked at Ron and Pete. He went to Amy, pulled paper towels out of the container, wet them and handed them to her, and left the water running in the sink so she could clean herself up.

"I'm sorry," she whispered as she rested her forehead on the back of her arm.

"Don't worry about. It's happened to all of us. You don't have to stay if you don't want to."

Amy stood and wiped her face again. "No," she said and shook her head. "I wanted to be involved in this."

She put on a clean apron and went back to where she'd been standing before. Zach tore off the soiled apron he wore and put on a clean one, then went to stand beside Amy and Ron.

Pete looked at Amy, then at Zach. Zach nodded and Pete continued. He placed the bat on another table and photographed it as well. Then he turned the body onto its back and continued the examination.

After cutting the leather strap from the neck, he placed it on the table with the bat and penis. Then he made a Y-shaped incision on the chest, cracked the sternum and sawed through the ribs, then lifted the whole section off and set it on the table next to the penis. He went through his usual routine of weighing the heart and liver, along with the rest of the organs, removing each one carefully. Drawing blood for a tox-screen, he reserved sections of tissue for analysis. There was considerable damage done inside the anal cavity by the baseball bat, but that was no surprise. Other than being dead, the body appeared to be in good health. The entire procedure was videotaped and the doctor's comments were recorded as he worked.

When he was done for the record, he turned off the video camera and recorder, then looked at Zach, Amy, and Ron. "Questions?"

Amy looked at Zach and Ron. Zach and Ron looked at each other.

"Thousands," Zach replied. "I just don't know where to start right now. Let me think about it all for a bit and I'll get back to you."

He looked up as Amy left the autopsy room. He sighed and followed her out.

"Are you all right?" Zach asked Amy when he stepped into the hallway and found her crouched on her heels with her back against the wall.

Pulling on her bottom lip, Amy mutely stared at the floor. After a few moments she looked up at Zach and nodded. "I wasn't expecting that," she said quietly.

"No way you could have," he said as he knelt in front of her. "I saw it out in the desert and still wasn't quite prepared for it. I could've warned you, I guess."

"You could have. Why didn't you?"

Zach looked at his big hands for a few seconds, examined the nails and shrugged. "I guess I wanted you to see it like I did the first time. No warning, just the full shock of it up close and personal. And maybe because I was hoping you'd see it and want to stay the hell out of my way until I've got you a suspect to prosecute."

She smiled at him then. "It didn't work."

Marie McGaha

He grinned. "I know." Standing, he offered his hand and she took it. "Come on," he said. "Let's get a cup of coffee."

~ Six ~

It had happened again, although it hadn't been her intention at all. She hadn't had the nightmares since she'd killed Clarence but then they'd started again without warning. Waking up in her bed, as sweat poured off her, a scream clotted in her throat, she stared wild-eyed into the darkness. She reached for the bedside lamp, switched it on and closed her eyes while she caught her breath. She thought it was over. She thought killing Clarence had killed the demons she'd felt chasing her for so long. She was wrong, and she didn't want this, didn't want the nightmares, and didn't want the knowledge that killing again would allow her nights of dreamless sleep.

She'd fought so hard to have a normal life, and she'd gone to such pains to change her life. She had left her hometown without a word, had gone to great lengths to change who she was, and no one knew anything else about her other than what she'd told them. All it had required was going to a cemetery and finding the headstone of a young child who had died years ago, someone who'd been born the same year she had but had only lived a few months. The information she'd needed was all right there on the stone, and she'd sent for a birth certificate, obtained a social security number, and set about changing her life. She closed the door completely on the life she had before with a new job, driver's license, credit cards, and then she'd enrolled in night school.

When she was younger she'd wanted to be

a lawyer but life had a vicious way of changing a person's plans. Now, however, she'd been able to go to law school, had been able to have her dreams come true. She'd fought for it. She'd lied for it, that was true, but she'd done all that was in her power for the chance to change her life. College hadn't been easy, but she had been determined. The late nights studying, the endless hours spent in the library, writing papers, being ready for midterms and finals—*that* she'd done on her own. No matter what else happened, she'd done that with no one's help and she was proud of herself.

She had been able to erase her horrid past, had been able to leave it behind her and become someone else. But she hadn't been able to leave those awful memories behind her. Those she couldn't outrun no matter how hard she tried. She dressed for success. The people in her office knew she was a good lawyer. They admired the way she went after criminals, how ruthless she was in prosecuting her cases. No one could find fault in her work. She was meticulous, making sure all the facts were laid out clearly and concisely for the jury. She could elicit emotions from the jurors—make them cry, make them angry, and make them laugh. She could make them doubt the defense, make them absolutely sure she was telling them how things had really happened. And she'd lost only one case, though it still haunted her.

Guilt or innocence wasn't a concern. If the police had any evidence at all, even if it was circumstantial, she could get a conviction. Her philosophy was if they weren't guilty of that particular crime, it only meant they'd gotten away with some other equally vicious crime. And if not that, they would eventually commit a crime if they weren't convicted of the one they were being tried for now. She had no illusions of innocence. There was no such thing and she slept peacefully after every conviction that was handed down. She slept peacefully for every life sentence, for every death penalty sentence rendered. She felt no guilt, no sorrow. She felt nothing for the men she'd made sure would never walk the streets again.

The only time she felt anything at all was when the nightmares came, and she had never had a night's peace until after she committed the first murder. It had been so wonderful to sleep peacefully night after night for all those weeks following the murder. She didn't like calling it murder. Murder was a heinous crime committed by criminals. What she had done wasn't murder. She had killed, that was true, but she wasn't a murderer.

Murderers killed at random, they killed for the fun of it, they killed for no reason at all. *She* was meting out justice no one had ever gone to the trouble to mete out for her. She was giving herself a measure of peace she'd never known before. She was preventing other women from the horrors these men enjoyed inflicting upon the weak and helpless. And yes, she admitted, she had been weak and she had been helpless but no more. She was strong now, she was sure of herself now, and she was sure that no man, no matter who he was, or what he said, would ever, ever make her weak again.

When she'd killed Clarence, it had been a fluke she'd even run across him at all. But after the nightmares began again, she knew what she had to do. She couldn't go hunting for Mark Abernathy, but she had access to computer systems the average person didn't. She had ways to find people who didn't want to be found and it had taken her less than fifteen minutes to find his current address, phone number, social security number, and place of employment. It had been so easy arranging the rest of it.

She'd seen it done within the police department. They had set up stings that rounded up numerous criminals in one fell swoop so she just copied their methods. She knew him—or had years and years ago in another lifetime—and she was betting he hadn't changed. She'd sent him an official looking letter telling him he'd won a Harley-Davidson motorcycle and all he had to do was appear in Phoenix to claim it. She'd even made the arrangements for his airfare and picked him up herself at the airport. The drive from Albuquerque to Phoenix wasn't far, and she'd managed to make all the arrangements for the weekend. It had worked out beautifully, and even though he thought he recognized her, he hadn't been able to make the connection.

She followed the same plan she had with Clarence, though she had made a few changes, like the area where she killed him. And the baseball bat. She wanted the punishment to fit the crime, and even though he'd done the time for raping and beating her, for leaving her for dead, it was hardly justice. He'd walked out of prison in less than five years.

Remembering sitting in court made her shudder with the thoughts of her face still swollen, eyes still hideous shades of black and blue that were beginning to turn to more hideous shades of green and yellow. Her lip had been cut and swollen but was now scabbed over, and the bruises from his hands were still faintly visible on her throat. Although the stitches where he'd stabbed her had been removed, the wound still pulled and ached.

He'd been more than rough, raping and sodomizing her with himself, with a pop bottle, with his hand and arm, over and over throughout the entire night. He'd called her horrible names, humiliated her by urinating on her, hit her with his fist, slapped her with an open hand, and whipped her with his belt. He brutalized her all night long and when she was too weak to scream, to even cry, he pulled a plastic bag over her head and taped it around her throat. Then he'd walked out of the cheap motel room and left her lying on the floor. If it hadn't been for the maid coming in early that morning, she would have died there as well.

Taking a deep breath, she blew it out slowly and calmed herself. Justice had been done. Finally. And the grand moment had been when she told him who she was and she saw the look of disbelief on his face and fear in his eyes. Then the realization that she was going to kill him had registered on his face and she grinned. She'd had to cut the baseball bat down but she didn't care, it was big enough to cause excruciating pain for him, not to mention internal damage. Now he knew what being sodomized really felt like, and she had listened to him beg, listened to him grovel, listened to him scream. And scream. She couldn't say she enjoyed doing it but she was satisfied with the results.

His eyes had nearly bulged out of their sockets as sweat poured off his body, and then she'd sat and waited, allowing the pain to settle firmly into his body, and more importantly, into his mind. She wanted him to know how he'd hurt her. She wanted him to understand what real fear was, what it felt like to be helpless, to be brutalized. She wanted him to understand what he'd done to her, how it felt to be at another person's mercy. Then, when he didn't seem to notice the pain any longer, she sliced off his penis and shoved it in his mouth, then tied the leather thong tightly around his neck. She should have used a plastic bag, she thought later, but it didn't really matter now. He was dead and the last thing he saw before he went to hell was her face. It was the only thing he'd see for all of eternity. Afterwards she'd gone through the process of cleaning up everything nice and neat. It was more than he'd done for her.

For now the nightmares had stopped. Another demon was dead.

She stood in the shower, letting the hot water stream down her back as she leaned her forehead against the wall, washing the stench of him off her. She washed the memories down the drain—let it all wash away. There'd never been anyone to help her, to save her, to hold her. She'd never had a safe place in her entire life. Now she was settling the score. Now they'd all pay for what they'd done to her and to every other woman they'd abused.

She knew somehow that Mark Abernathy was just a quick fix and soon the nightmares would begin again, but she could wait. She knew who would be next, and a smile curved her lips as she thought of him. He'd fooled her more than once. His intentions had been dark and evil and she'd not been able to see through them. But now... now, she knew what she would do next. Unlike that SOB, *her* intentions were perfectly clear, and she'd be getting a little closure on that chapter too. She took a deep breath and smiled.

~ Seven ~

"Oh, please, Ellison." Amy looked at him and he knew she didn't believe him.

"It's true, I swear." He laughed at the look on her face.

She shook her head. "Well, you'll have to prove that to me."

"So you've never been on a ranch or a farm?"

"Never."

"Then why do you think it's not true?"

"Because... I mean, *how*?" She wrinkled her nose.

Zach shrugged. "If it wasn't that big, the bull would never be able to impregnate the cow. Bovine vagina is deep." He held out his arm and gestured. "I have to put my arm in to the shoulder when I do artificial inseminations."

When she squinted, he knew Amy still wasn't sure if he was telling the truth.

"That's disgusting," she said. "You stick your arm in there?"

He nodded, totally enjoying making her so uncomfortable. "It has to be done sometimes if you want a certain result, or if the bull doesn't do his job."

Amy still wasn't sure if she believed him or not. "Okay, I'll take your word for it... for now," she added with a smile.

They were eating lunch together in the park. They had spent weeks going at each other, arguing every time they were together, but had finally come to the realization that they really did like each other. The newly formed friendship hadn't gone any further than the occasional work hour lunch, but they were both aware something more was developing between them. Friendship was all they'd acknowledge because neither one had been willing to admit they might want more, nor were they willing to be the first to take the next step.

Zach liked being with her, occasionally. More than the casual lunch would be too much to handle since she still lit a fire in him every time he laid eyes on her. And he could sense Amy wasn't ready to get closer to him, or to any man. She'd suffered through a bad marriage and a worse divorce, and she wasn't ready to take even one step that might lead in that direction.

They picked up the remains of their lunch, dropped it into one of the cans chained to a post and walked back to the office building. The District Attorney's offices were in a building on Lomas Boulevard next door to the courthouse, and Zach watched as Amy went through the smoky glass doors. Then he turned and walked down the street, turned right and walked the two blocks to the five-story building on Roma Street that housed the law enforcement offices. He looked at Ellen sitting at her desk as he walked into his office and she raised her eyebrows at him.

"Nice lunch?" she asked.

"Yep," he muttered as he shut the door before she could comment further.

At his desk, he opened the file on Mark Abernathy and glanced over it again. He knew it by heart, he'd read it so many times.

He wasn't getting anywhere, and the

information he'd requested from California
hadn't yet been faxed. That was only one
commonality—both of the victims were from
California. Both had also done time in the
California prison system, both had been drug
addicts, both had sponged off women on welfare,
and both had been killed in basically the same
manner. There had to be more than coincidence
alone.

Ellen came into Zach's office without
knocking and handed over the faxes that had just
come in for him. Thanking her, he looked over
the list of women Abernathy had dated, lived
with, been married to, or had kids with. Then
Zach pulled the Broom file out of the cabinet and
found the list of women compiled for him. Laying
both lists side-by-side, he scrutinized the
information, but none of the names matched.
Zach drew a deep breath and went over it again,
and then he picked up the phone and began
dialing 4-1-1 and compiling phone numbers for as
many of the women as he could.

He had already run their names through
NCIC, but the National Criminal Information
Center had only shown three of the women had a
record, and he'd ordered the rap sheets to be
faxed. None of them had any serious beefs—
shoplifting, misdemeanor marijuana possession,
but nothing more serious. He knew in his gut that
they weren't the ones he was looking for, but he
also knew the one he was looking for was there.
He could feel it, but he just wasn't seeing it for
some reason.

Rubbing his eyes, he looked at his watch,
sighed and put the files away. It was time he

went home.

~ * ~

"Hey, Earl," Zach greeted the dog as he walked into the house a short while later. After taking a shower, he pulled on a pair of clean Levi's and a T-shirt, then put on his Nikes. Digging through the refrigerator, he found nothing appetizing. Restlessness assaulted him and wouldn't let the murder cases rest. The information just kept spinning through his head, so he decided to drive back into town for dinner, and maybe a movie as well. He knew he had to do something to clear his head, get his mind off the cases so he could come back to them with a fresh perspective.

~ * ~

Seeing Zach at a table alone when she walked into the pub, Amy walked over to him. "Hi, Zach."

"Amy," he said with a grin. "What are you doing here?"

"I was supposed to meet my friend, Sam, but something came up at the last minute and she couldn't make it. I didn't feel like going back home." Amy shrugged.

"Want to sit?"

She pulled out the chair and sat. "Thanks."

"How are things over at the D.A.'s office?" Zach asked.

"Oh, you know, same as usual." Amy shifted uncomfortably in her chair. Zach looked at her in a way that made her squirm. She didn't know why the man could pull her in so many different ways at once. He caused heat to slide through her gut, caused the hairs on the back of her neck to stand on end, caused her blood pressure to rise, and her heart rate to increase. She hadn't had this reaction to a man in so long she'd nearly forgotten what it was like.

And Zach frightened her. Not that she was afraid of him in the sense that he'd physically hurt her, but she was sure he could put her emotions and her heart both at serious risk. If she hadn't felt such attraction to him, or liked him so much, maybe she would consider sleeping with him, but something inside of her told her taking a step like that with Zach Ellison would be a permanent one. She wasn't sure if she was ready to go there.

"So," she said while nervously playing with her fingers in her lap. "Have you come up with anything on the case?"

~ * ~

"I haven't found what I'm looking for, but I know it's there. I feel it every time I look at the case files. There's something right in front of me, but I just can't quite put my finger on it." Zach thought she looked as nervous as he felt, but he'd take a few minutes to let her settle down before he guided this conversation around to where he wanted it to go. He needed another beer and thought Amy could use a drink herself. Signaling the waitress, he ordered another mug of beer and Amy ordered an apple martini. When the waitress turned away from their table, he cleared his throat.

"Maybe if you let me look it over with you I'll see something you don't."

Zach picked up a menu. "Maybe," he

answered. "What do you want to eat?"

"Oh, I..."

"You've got to eat, Amy." Zach handed her his menu. She smiled as she took it. "We can be friends at times other than lunch," he told her.

She looked at him over the top of the menu and swallowed hard. "I know."

"Good and after we eat I'll take you out to my ranch and show you the cows," he said with a mischievous grin. "Not afraid to be alone with me are you?" Zach asked, bringing the mug of beer to his lips and draining the last of it just as the waitress set new drinks before them.

"Are you ready to order or would you like a few more minutes?" The waitress looked at Zach and smiled seductively.

"I'll have the roast beef sandwich," Zach answered.

The waitress's smile faded as she looked expectantly at Amy. "I'll have the chef's salad with ranch on the side." The waitress took the menu and walked away.

"So?" Zach put both hands on the table.

"So... what?"

A slow grin played across Zach's mouth. "Are you afraid to be alone with me?"

Amy swallowed half her martini. "No, of course not. I just thought maybe you'd be busy tonight," she lied.

"Hey, you two." Rick Sanchez sauntered up to their table.

"Hi, Rick," Amy said with a sigh with relief at the interruption. She didn't know why she was so jumpy this evening since she and Zach had been getting along so well at work. Perhaps that was it, she decided—she didn't have the safety of her office to go to after spending only an hour with him. Being together during work was safe, and having dinner with him was not. After lunch she could walk away from him, but here, now, there was no safe place. And it was definitely not safe for her to be alone with Zach. She couldn't deny her attraction to him was growing. Taking a breath, she smiled at Rick then looked at Zach.

"Is this a private party or can anyone join in?" Rick laughed, but looked pointedly at Zach.

Zach recognized the look, it was jealousy and it was a challenge. Zach set his beer down on the table and his mouth curved in a slow, lazy grin. "It looks private to me... *Rick.*"

"Well," he said, tipping back his bottle of beer. "I have to be getting on home anyway." He turned without saying good-bye and walked out of the restaurant.

"That was rude." Amy looked at Zach, not even trying to hide her smile.

Zach shrugged and finished his beer. "It was. He could've at least said good-bye."

Amy chuckled. "I meant you."

Zach shrugged and took a drink of his beer. "I don't like him."

"Why not?"

"Call it a gut feeling." Zach grinned at her. *Or call it one man protecting what he thinks is his from another man who wants it,* he thought and glanced out the window to where Rick was climbing into his car.

~ * ~

Amy sat in the passenger seat of Zach's

truck as they drove out of town. She was up against the door as if sitting any closer to him would be dangerous. She knew it was silly, she was a grown woman and it wasn't as if she was a virgin. But something about Zachariah Ellison made her jumpy and nervous, and she hoped he didn't think that her going with him to see his ranch wasn't the same as saying yes to going to bed with him.

Not knowing what she wanted, or didn't want, wasn't helping either. She knew she was attracted to him, but she had been raised right, raised in church, and sleeping around wasn't something she did. It had actually been years since she'd had intimate relations with a man. Then again, Sam had told her that Zach hadn't been with another woman since his wife died, so maybe he was raised with those same values. She hoped so.

And she knew she couldn't just have casual sex with a man, knowing it would mean nothing to him, knowing he expected it to mean nothing to her as well. The first time she'd had sex was at her high school graduation party with Bobby Woodford, her boyfriend of two years. Everyone had expected them to get married, but after that summer together between high school and college, they had just drifted apart and their relationship seemed so... *high school*.

During her senior year of college, she fell in love with Andrew Winston, III, and within a year they'd married. He was from a very wealthy Monterey family and even though Amy didn't quite fit in, she'd tried because she loved Andrew so much. But by the time they'd been married three years, she knew he was having an affair, and by year four they were separated. During year five the divorce was filed. It had been a huge mistake that Amy didn't plan on repeating.

~ * ~

Zach swung the Avalanche off the pavement and onto the narrow one-lane dirt road that was his driveway. He drove slowly to the house and parked by the back door. It was still light out and Amy could see the house, barns, and out buildings, as well as the black dog trotting toward the truck.

"That's Earl," Zach told her. "He's not dangerous. Unless you're a cookie."

Amy laughed and opened her door. Earl came around the truck and she extended the back of her hand to him.

"Hey, Earl," she said to him. "You look like a friendly dog. What do you think? Do you like me?"

Earl wagged his tail, then sat back on his haunches and lifted a paw to her. Amy laughed and shook it.

"He likes you," Zach said with a laugh. "Come inside. Hey, Earl, you want a cookie?"

Earl bounded up the back steps and waited for Zach to open the door. Zach held the door for Amy and, once inside, gave Earl a doggie biscuit.

Zach went into the kitchen with Amy behind him. "Would you like a cup of coffee?"

"Sure, if you've got decaf. If not, I'm fine."

"Decaf it is then," he said and went about making the pot of coffee. He nodded toward the table. "Don't be bashful, take a seat."

Amy sat down at the kitchen table. It was piled with papers, folders, and various cases Zach was working on, including a copy of the files on both Broom and Abernathy. Zach glanced over at her, saw her looking at the brown folders and knew she wanted to take a look.

"Go ahead," he said.

Amy jumped. "What?"

Zach laughed. "Go ahead and look at it, I know you want to."

"Are you sure?"

Zach shrugged. "What, didja think I brought you here for sex?"

"Of course not." She flipped open the file and began to read, not even noticing when Zach set a cup of coffee next to her. Something told her he was right, the answer was right there, but she couldn't quite work the pieces around to fit exactly the right way. She looked at Zach's notes, then at Pete's.

"I think that's right," she said looking across the table at Zach.

"What is?"

"Your suspicion. Pete's suspicion. You're both right about it being a woman."

"And how do you know that?"

She shrugged. "You won't believe me."

"Try me."

"I can see it, or rather, I can feel it," she said as she looked up at him.

A smile played at Zach's mouth. "What? Like you're psychic or something?"

Amy tilted her head to one side and smiled at him. "No, I'm not psychic or something. But I've read the profiles and I've read the rap sheets. Don't you see it? Both of these guys prey on women, use them, abuse them, and throw them away. One does it out right; the other does it by ambush." She shook her head. "And I don't blame whoever it was either. These guys deserved what they got, and I can see why she did it."

Zach laughed out loud then. "And you're the one who's going to prosecute this case?"

She grinned and closed the files. "Don't tell my boss I said that, okay?"

Zach stood and reached for her. "Come with me." With only a moment's hesitation, she took his hand.

"Where are we going?"

"Leave the files, Amy, we're not at work now. Take a walk with me."

He led her outside, across the yard, and they walked away from the lights of the house. The moonless sky was black velvet lined with millions of bright, twinkling diamonds.

"It's beautiful, Zach. I never get to see the sky like this where my house is. There are too many lights from the city. Do you own all of this?"

He chuckled. "Not all of it. I have five hundred acres and about two hundred head of cattle, and forty-eight horses. And Earl, of course. Do you ride?"

"I rode a horse once when I was younger. A friend of mine had one when I was in junior high, but I don't think you could actually say I ride."

"Then I'll have to teach you." He stopped and turned toward her. She was so beautiful, he thought, and reached out to take a lock of her hair between his fingers. He was nervous and took a calming breath. It had been so long since he'd felt this way, and looking at her now, he could feel his heart racing, his blood thrumming through his veins. He knew every word they'd said to one another, every look they'd given each other, had been leading to this moment. He smiled and let his hand drop from her hair to her shoulder, gently resting there.

"Amy, nothing is going to happen here unless you want it to," he said softly as he bent his head toward her.

~ * ~

She tilted her head back, looked up at him, felt her heart thud in her chest, and then his mouth was on hers and she was climbing all over him. All those years alone, all those nights of wishing she had someone to hold her, all those weeks working with Zach. The wanting of him, the needing of him, the denying of what she had been feeling—it all came pouring out of her at that moment of contact.

Her arms wound around his neck, her fingers worked furiously through his hair, over his shoulders, kneading his neck. She could feel his hands on her face, his fingers burning into her skin, his lips sizzling against hers as his tongue probed deep inside her mouth, encouraging her to take more of him, to give more to him.

She couldn't think for the blood pounding in her head, couldn't breathe because her breath had caught in her chest. She could only feel. She could feel his hands moving from her face, trailing down her neck, felt them move over her shoulders and down her back. She had never been so aware of her own body in her life, had never been so aware of another person.

Then he pulled away, took a step back and dropped his hands to his sides. He was panting, his chest heaving as he tried to catch his breath. They stood there looking at each other for a long moment, neither speaking. Zach raked his hands through his hair, took a deep breath and blew it out. He stepped toward her, took her hands in his and brought them both to his mouth, and kissed them gently.

"I—" He paused and took another breath. "I haven't been with a woman since my wife died. I haven't wanted a woman since my wife died. Not until I met you. Still, I didn't expect to feel what I just felt when we kissed. So I'm going to give you the chance right now, Amy. If you don't plan on staying, tell me now and I'll take you home. But if you come back inside with me, don't ask me to stop and don't ask me to take you home, because I won't." He dropped her hands and looked into her eyes and waited.

She took a deep breath, fixed her gaze on a distant spot in the semi-darkness, chewed on her bottom lip as both fear and desire warred within her. Then she took his hand in hers and led him back to the house.

He held the door for her, then lifted her into his arms and carried her to his bedroom. Setting her on her feet, he turned on the bedside lamp, letting it cast soft, golden light into the room. Then he turned toward Amy, reached for a lock of her hair, and let it slide through his fingers. He gently guided one finger along her jaw line. She was nervous, he could tell, but then, so was he.

She stroked her fingers lightly over his chest while he recovered. She didn't want to say anything, didn't want to break the spell cast by their lovemaking, but she was so full of the love she felt for him, she wanted to tell him. She bit her tongue and kept it to herself. She knew men needed time, and he'd probably just think her foolish anyway; people didn't just fall in love because they had sex together.

That must be what it is, she thought, *just the emotions of finally breaking this celibate state. And what girl wouldn't think herself in love with a man like Zach Ellison?*

"You're quiet," Zach said after a while.

"Just thinking I should be getting home," she answered.

"Why?"

"Well, I just thought…" She trailed off.

"You just thought you'd seduce me then run off and leave me here alone, huh?"

She laughed. "I just didn't want to keep you from getting some sleep since we both have to get up early in the morning."

"Do you remember what I told you before this started?" He didn't let her reply. "I told you if you came back inside with me, not to ask me to take you home because I won't. You're not leaving now."

"Really? I do have to go home eventually you know. We do have to go to work in the morning."

"No, we don't. We can call in, take a day off and lay in bed all day."

"Zach, I have cases to work on."

"Do you have to be in court tomorrow?"

"No, not tomorrow."

"Then it's settled." He brushed her hair away from her face and caressed her cheek, then slanted his mouth over hers and kissed her softly.

"I need you to stay," he said hoarsely.

She kissed him back and nodded. "I need to stay."

~ Eight ~

The next morning, both called in to work and took a personal day. For Zach it was the first time he'd ever taken a day off in the middle of the week.

While Zach cooked bacon, eggs, and toast, Amy looked over the case files again.

There is a woman behind all of this, a very gutsy one, Amy thought. One that had more guts than she did and one that had been hurt beyond anything Amy could comprehend. She knew the connection between the two men was here in the files. She just couldn't put her finger on it.

Zach set the plates on the table. "Put it away, Amy, we're not working today."

She looked up at him and smiled as she flipped the folder closed. "Okay, okay." She picked up her fork and dug into the pile of eggs scrambled with green onions and jalapenos. "Mmmm, these are good," she told him.

"Thanks, I do all right in the kitchen since I've had to cook for myself most of my life."

"Got any salsa and sour cream?"

He looked at her. "Really?"

She nodded through a mouthful of eggs, then washed it down with coffee. He went to the refrigerator and retrieved salsa and sour cream and set them on the table. He watched while she poured salsa over her eggs and then plopped a big spoonful of sour cream on top, grinning when she took a big bite.

"What?" She looked at him.

"Nothing. We've just eaten lunch together about thirty times and all I've ever seen you eat is a salad or yogurt or a piece of fruit. I didn't think you ate real food."

"Ha, little do you know. I eat that stuff for lunch because it's convenient for me to take to work. But as soon as I get home, I raid the fridge."

He grinned and shook his head. They both settled in to finish their breakfasts, and then Zach set their plates in the sink.

"Come on." He took her hand. "Let's saddle up and I'll teach you how to ride."

"Oh, I don't know, Zach," she said nervously.

"Don't worry, I've got an old mare named Sally you can ride. She's gentle as a kitten and you'll be safe."

"Okay, if you say so."

He gathered her into his arms and kissed her gently. "I say so."

~ * ~

They walked out into the bright sunshine and Zach gave Earl a cookie. The dog followed the pair to the barn where the two hired hands were bucking hay from the loft. The men looked at Zach, at Amy, and then at each other. They'd worked for Zach for nearly five years and he knew they had never seen a woman at his house, nor had they ever known Zach to be home in the middle of the week.

"Luke, John, this is Amy. Amy, these guys work for me." He saw the look on their faces as they nodded and mumbled hello to Amy. Then they just stood staring. "Well, they used to work for me anyway," Zach said and raised an eyebrow at them. They went back to work.

Zach grabbed two saddles and threw them in the back of his old farm truck. "Grab the tack there, Amy," he told her. She looked at the wall and then looked back at him with a blank look on her face.

Zach grinned. "You really don't know anything about horses, do you?"

She shook her head. "Not really."

"Okay, but that's got to change. I can't live with a woman who doesn't know her way around a horse." He grabbed the tack they needed and threw it in the back of the truck with the saddles. "Let's go."

Amy stared at him like he was purple and had horns. He tilted his head, not knowing what had gotten into her, then walked over to her. "Are you all right?"

"Um, yeah," she stammered.

"Then get in the truck," he ordered and swatted her lightly on the rear.

He opened the door and she got in, then he hopped into the driver's seat and fired up the engine, pulled out of the barnyard and steered toward the pasture. Earl barked and when Zach slowed, he jumped into the back of the truck.

~ * ~

Amy stared out the window, deep in thought. He'd said, "live with a woman", as in living with her? No, she must've misunderstood what he'd said, or he'd just been teasing her because she knew nothing about horses. He couldn't have been serious. She rolled it over and over in her head, analyzing it to death, while her heart pounded in her chest and her blood pumped wildly. *No, it couldn't be what it sounded like,* she decided. She was just being silly. Zach couldn't possibly be thinking about living with her, could he?

No, of course not.

She shook her head at her own silliness.

The truck bumped along over the uneven land until they came to the gate and Zach jumped out to open it. Driving through, he stopped again to shut it behind them.

"The horses are probably out on the west side where the pond is. They'll probably ignore us, but the cattle will come when they hear the truck because they'll think I'm bringing hay even though they know it's not feeding time. Just hearing the truck brings them over, sort of like Pavlov's dog."

They drove along slowly, went over a small hill, then the valley spread out before them with a large pond sparkling in the sun. The horses grazed nearby and the cattle were forming a single line as they came toward the truck. Amy was amazed at the sight, but when the cattle pressed around the truck, she became alarmed.

Zach clapped his hands and shouted at them. Earl jumped to the ground and began barking at the animals. They paid the dog no mind, but one of them tried to kick him as he nipped at its heels. Zach pushed on their rumps to move them out of the way so he could get to Amy's door and open it for her.

"Don't be afraid of them, just push them out of your way. They won't hurt you." But he held her hand tightly in his as he led her through the herd. He had two bridles in his other hand

and they walked together toward the pond and the horses with some of the cattle following them.

"They're kind of cute," Amy said with a giggle. "They just follow along like puppies or something."

Zach laughed. "Yeah, real cute." He whistled loudly and the horses looked up. "See the gray one with the white mane and tail? That's Sally. She's about fifteen years old and very gentle. She's worthless as an old boot really, but I've had her since she was a baby. She's given me some good stock though, so she'll live out her life here. The black one there is Demon. He's mine."

"Is he mean?"

"No, not mean, just determined to do things his way. He's four and all of the foals there are his. Every time a mare comes in season, Demon is there to do his job. He's a stud from champion lines, but he has this idea no one is going to ride him. He nearly killed me when I first started training him to the saddle and then tried to ride him the first few times."

"And you still rode him?"

"Of course. If I hadn't stayed on him he would have gotten really mean," Zach said with a grin. "This way he's just slightly unbearable."

They walked until they were by the pond and Amy stayed where she was while Zach bridled Sally and led the old horse over to her.

"Just hold onto the reins and I'll get Demon," he said.

Amy took the reins and looked at the horse. She timidly reached up and touched Sally's head. "Okay, Sally, you seem nice enough," Amy told the horse. "I don't suppose you can understand me, can you?"

The horse nodded her head. Amy jumped. The horse did not just answer her. Amy squinted and looked into the horse's eyes.

"Can you understand me?" The horse nodded again. "Well, then, I guess you should know I don't know how to ride, but Zach tells me you're very gentle. I'll try to be gentle too, so maybe we'll get along with each other."

She stopped when she heard Zach laughing. He had just walked up, leading Demon.

"How long have you been there?" Amy asked with a sheepish grin.

"Long enough to hear you talking to a horse like she knows what you're saying."

"Are you so sure she can't? I asked her if she could and she nodded." Amy put her hands on her hips.

Zach continued laughing. "Well, if she said she understands, then I guess she can."

Amy held his gaze. "You're making fun of me."

"No, darlin', I'm not making fun of you. I'm having fun *with* you. Watch this." He came around to Sally's head and stroked the horse's neck. "Hey ol' girl, are you doing all right today?" The horse nodded. "Do you want to go for a ride?" The horse nodded again.

Amy's mouth dropped open. "She really does understand."

Zach laughed. "Sally, do you want to wear a tutu and walk on water?"

The horse nodded and Amy laughed out loud.

"You see," Zach explained, "she just responds to the sound of a human voice. It doesn't matter what anyone says—she just nods. She's always been like that. I don't why. Horses are peculiar animals."

Leading the two horses to the pickup truck, Zach began saddling them. He saddled Sally first and explained the process to Amy, letting her help with the cinch. Then he showed her how to mount the horse and then adjusted the stirrups for her shorter legs. He saddled Demon quickly while the horse snorted and pawed the ground. After mounting the animal, he waited patiently while Demon pranced around in a circle, and then reared up on his hind legs. Amy squealed. Zach laughed.

"Don't be afraid, Amy. No matter what Demon does, Sally won't be bothered by it. Now hold the reins in your right hand kind of loose, but don't drop them. Cluck your tongue and lightly tap your heels to her flanks."

Amy did as she was told and Sally obligingly began to walk forward. Demon wasn't as happy to be walking along at such a slow pace.

"Amy, just keep walking Sally in that direction," Zach told her and pointed. "I'm going to run Demon a little ways to get some of this antsiness out of him. I won't go far—you'll be able to see me. If I don't let him have his head, he'll be in a bad mood all afternoon."

Amy nodded and Zach tapped Demon with his heels. Demon was off like a shot with Zach leaning low in the saddle.

Amy watched horse and rider with awe. She'd never seen anything like it in her life. It was like a dance, she thought. The horse was fast and sure, his muscles bunching and stretching, and his black hide was sleek and shiny in the sunlight. Sally continued to walk at a slow pace and Amy adjusted to the feel of the movement beneath her.

This is nice, she decided. *A little faster would be nice, too.*

She clucked her tongue and nudged Sally with her heels. Sally obliged and began to trot. Amy screamed and bailed off the horse, landing on the ground flat on her back. Sally came back to her and nudged Amy with her nose.

Getting to her feet, Amy dusted herself off. Sally nudged her again.

"Thanks," Amy told the horse and patted Sally's head as she picked up the reins. "Okay, let's try this again."

She put her foot in the stirrup, grabbed the saddle horn and hauled herself onto the saddle, feeling very satisfied with herself. She reached out and patted Sally. She tapped her heels to Sally's flanks again, and the horse began to walk. Amy took a deep breath and tapped Sally again, a little harder this time, and the horse began to trot. This time Amy bounced up and down, giggling the entire way.

"I can ride, Zach, did you see? I rode her while she ran."

Zach laughed. "I saw, Amy. You did real good."

Zach had been watching the whole time and smiled at the way she bounced around in the saddle, gripping the reins in one hand and the saddle horn tightly with the other. He had seen her fall and almost raced to her side, but then she'd gotten to her feet and seemed to be okay, so he stayed back to see if she'd get back on. He was pleased when she did. He rode over to her and pulled Demon to a walk beside Amy and Sally.

They rode side by side for the better part of an hour, then Zach brought Demon to a halt and told Amy she'd want to walk for a little ways as well so she didn't get sore. They walked hand in hand, leading the horses behind them.

"Have you always lived here?" Amy asked him.

"I moved here after Stacie died. I owned the land before I met her, but she didn't want to live in the middle of nowhere, so we bought a house in town. I kept the horses and cattle out here and spent what time I could here. After she got sick, I was here less and less, and when she died, I sold the house in town and built the one here."

"I'm sorry about your wife, Zach. I've heard the stories from people in the office."

"Yeah, I guess there isn't much that doesn't get spread around from office to office. Small world." They walked in silence for a ways.

"Amy." Zach looked at her. "If there's anything you want to know, you can ask."

She looked at him and shrugged. "No, I don't think there is."

"I just thought women were bothered by things like that. Being with a man whose wife had died."

"I don't know. It's a little strange to me if

I think about it. I think if she was still alive we wouldn't be having this conversation. If I think that because of your pain in losing her I get to be with you, then it seems a little weird."

Zach said nothing for a moment. "What about you?" He looked at her. "You have any ex's or currents?"

She smiled up at him and shook her head. "No currents, one ex."

"I guess the rumor mill doesn't include you."

"I've never told anyone. I like my privacy and have no desire for anyone to talk about me or my past."

"So you were married?"

"I was. He was a spoiled little rich boy I met in college and fell in love with, or thought I did anyway. He had everything in life I'd never had, and I think it was the idea he was interested in me out of all the women he had to choose from that appealed to me. Made me feel special, and kind of blinded me to who he really was. We were married for five years and he'd been sleeping with other women for at least three of those years that I knew of. Probably longer. Anyway, we split up and I finished school and we haven't seen each other since."

"And no one since then?"

"Oh, I've had a few dates, but while I was in school there wasn't time for dates, and now I just work and go home."

"So I don't have to kick Rick's butt then?" He grinned.

"Rick? Oh please."

"Are you hungry?"

"I am," she said with a smile.

"Me, too." He dropped Demon's reins and wrapped his arms around Amy's waist. He'd meant only to hold her briefly and kiss her lightly, but when their lips met, desire shot straight through him.

Breaking the kiss, he could see the same desire in her eyes that he felt in his soul. He pulled a rolled up blanket from behind his saddle, and spread it on the ground in the shade of a tree. Bringing her to him, he kissed her again, then lowered them both to the blanket.

"I thought you were hungry?" he said breathlessly.

"I am," she said just as breathlessly.

"Then why did you seduce me? I wanted to get some food. You're shameless."

She laughed and slapped at him. "Yeah, *I'm* the shameless one."

"I don't know, Amy, when I tell the guys about this around the water cooler, maybe you'll learn to let a man eat when he wants to."

She rolled over on top of him. "Really? When I tell the girls in the office what a scoundrel you really are your reputation will be ruined."

He kissed her long and slow, and then said, "And when you tell the girls in the office about me, be sure to mention I'm great in bed, okay?"

She laughed. "You're horrible. Now feed me."

They dressed and rode the horses back to the truck. Zach unsaddled Sally and handed Amy a curry brush. "You have to brush a horse after every ride," he told her. "It makes them feel better and cools them down."

Amy brushed every inch of Sally while Zach unsaddled Demon, and then curried the black horse, which snorted and whinnied the entire time. When they were done, Zach whistled and Earl came loping to him, his tongue lolling out of his mouth. The dog had been swimming in the pond and his fur was soaking wet. He sprayed Zach and Amy both when he shook himself off, then jumped into the back of the pick-up while Amy and Zach slid into the cab. Amy sat next to the door again, but Zach reached for her hand and pulled her to him.

"I want you to sit next to me," he said as he turned the vehicle around and rested his hand on her leg. "Let's take a shower when we get back to the house and get dressed up. I want to take you out to some place nice. We'll dance and eat by candle light, what do you think?"

"I don't have any clothes at your house, remember?"

"Okay, then I'll grab a change of clothes and we'll go by your house and shower there." He looked at her. "Okay?"

She nodded. "Okay."

They went ininside and Amy waited in the kitchen while Zach went into the bedroom to get his clothes. Fingering the files on the table again, she looked up to make sure Zach couldn't see her, and then opened the file. She put both Broom's and Abernathy's lists of women they'd had relationships with side by side and looked them over again. She knew it was there, knew it was a woman who knew them both, but none of the names matched up. Somehow they were missing it, and it was beginning to really bug her.

"Can't leave it alone, can you? You shoulda been a cop." Zach came back in the room with a plastic encased suit thrown over his shoulder.

"I know it's there, Zach, I just know it. I can feel it."

"I know. I get the same feeling when I look at it, but I just can't quite put my finger on it. Come on, let's get going, I'm starved."

They climbed into the Avalanche and Amy didn't sit by the door this time. She was beside Zach with her hand on his leg, and his hand on hers'. They drove down the dirt driveway and turned onto the paved road. They hadn't driven more than two miles when Amy squealed.

"Zach. Oh my God, I've got it."

"What? You've got what?"

"Turn around, turn around. We've got to go back to your house. I know why we couldn't make the connection."

Zach made a U-turn in the middle of the road and headed back to his house.

"Are you sure?" Zach opened the door for her and tossed Earl a cookie on his way in.

"I'm sure, Zach. I knew it was there, and it's been driving me crazy. It's one of the women on the list."

"I thought so too, but none of the names match. I've even seen rap sheets on some of them, but I haven't been able to come up with a suspect."

"I know, but there's some names missing

on Abernathy's list. Look." She flipped open the file on the table. "This list has the names of the women Broom lived with or was married to or whatever, and so does the list for Abernathy, but what we don't have is the list of women Abernathy raped or assaulted. And I bet when we have it, we'll find a name that matches one of the women on Broom's list."

Zach thumbed through the file until he found Abernathy's rap sheet, then he dialed the phone. He spoke to Ellen for a few minutes, asked her to pull up some records and compared them to the names he had. Then he hung up.

Zach shook his head. "None of the names they gave me are the same as any on Broom's list, Amy."

She sat heavily in a chair. "I'm sorry Zach. I was so sure I was right."

"I know darlin'. But I think you're on the right track anyway. I'll dig into it a little more tomorrow. Come on, let's get something to eat."

~ Nine ~

"Where have you been?" Samantha asked as Amy walked into the office the next morning.

Amy shrugged. "I took a day off."

"Just like that, for no reason at all?"

"Yeah, just like that."

"Rumor has it Zach Ellison took a day off just like that as well," Samantha said coyly.

"Hmm, I suppose he can do what he wants."

"So, the fact the two of you both took the same day off for no particular reason is just coincidence?"

As she walked to her office, Amy replied, "Absolutely." She shut the door behind her, leaving Samantha to wonder exactly what was going on with her friend.

Amy spent the day in court going through arraignment after arraignment, bored out of her mind. She didn't want to be in court, she wanted to be with Zach, but she knew that was impossible. For now. They had made plans to meet at her house after work and then go out for the dinner they'd missed the night before. They'd wound up eating pizza and pouring over the case files instead.

The day just seemed to drag by, but finally five o'clock arrived and Amy didn't even stop to say good-bye to Samantha.

Amy arrived at her house before Zach did and decided she didn't want to go out to dinner. She wanted dinner in where they would have the privacy she wanted. She wasn't ready to share him, or the feelings she had for him just yet. She planned on feeding him, dancing with him, and then just being with him, and there was no need to go anywhere.

Dropping her briefcase on the floor by the front door, she picked up the phone, called her favorite restaurant and ordered dinner to go. She ran back out to her car and pulled out of the driveway—dinner would be ready by the time she got there.

~ * ~

They sat on the living room floor with the food from the restaurant on the coffee table between them. "Did you get any more information on Broom or Abernathy yet?" Amy asked through a bite of rice.

Zach shook his head as he forked another bite of honey-grilled salmon into his mouth. "No, but I have Ron Petrie digging into the backgrounds of both men more thoroughly. I feel just as strongly as you do about the connection between them being a woman. It's just a matter of finding her."

"What happens then?"

"We question her and see what she has to say." He shrugged. "It is possible that even though we find her she might not be the killer. Hopefully though, she'll have some useful information." Zach heard his beeper going off, and searched the room until he found it on the bar. "It's Petrie. Where's your phone?"

Amy pointed to the cordless phone on the end table by the recliner. Zach sat in the chair and dialed Ron's number.

"What?" Zach said into the mouthpiece.

"Where are you? I called you at the office,

called you at home, called your cell—it never takes me that many tries to get a hold of you."

"Don't worry about where I am. What do you want?"

"I got a hit on the names, thought you'd want to know."

"A hit? As in two of the same names?"

Ron grinned. "Yep. Abigail Suzanne Johnson. She cohabitated with Broom and she was one of Abernathy's rape victims. He weaseled out of the attempted murder charge, but picked up a dime on the assault and rape, then paroled five years later."

"Where is she?"

"No one knows. We're trying to get a location on her now."

Zach blew out a breath. "Good work, Ron. I'll see you in the morning." He hung up the phone.

"What?" Amy asked excitedly.

Zach grinned. "We were right, baby. We've got a common name for both cases."

Amy got up off the floor and practically jumped across the room, landing on his lap. "You're kidding?" Zach shook his head. "You're not kidding. Oh my gosh, Zach, this is awesome. Who is she?"

"Her name is Abigail Johnson. She lived with Broom and was a victim of Abernathy's. Ron doesn't have a location on her yet, but it shouldn't take long to find her."

"Oh. My. Gosh. This is awesome," Amy squealed again.

"Yes, it is. It's the first break we've had in this case," Zach said with a shake of his head.

"It's the *only* break we've had." He kissed her then, long and slow.

~ * ~

After finishing dinner, they took the rest of the bottle of the champagne and their glasses to the bedroom. Zach sat with his back against the headboard, leaning against a pillow with Amy between his legs leaning against his belly.

"Amy, there's something I want to talk to you about," he said.

"Mmm, hmm," she moaned slightly with her eyes closed. She was so comfortable with him, she didn't want to move.

"I wanted to ask if you'd, well, I would like it very much if you'd move in with me."

Amy's eyes flew open and she jerked up right, catching Zach on the chin with her head.

"A simple *no* would suffice." He rubbed his chin and laughed.

Amy moved from between his legs and turned around to face him. "Zach, isn't this a little fast?"

He shrugged. "Probably, but I know what I want, and I want you."

"Oh, Zach, you already have me. I don't know if living together is something I'm ready to do. I wasn't even ready for you."

"I don't mean to rush you into something you're not ready for. I forget sometimes how much older I am than you. When you get to be my age, little girl," he said in his best old man voice, "you'll understand when you find what you want, you don't wait for it to come to you."

Amy laughed and leaned into him. "You are so wise." She kissed him and he flipped her over on her back and pinned her hands above her head, while pinning both her legs with one of his. He lowered his head to hers and kissed her passionately.

"I love you, Amy."

She stared at him. "You do?"

Zach laughed. "You looked shocked."

"I am. I thought, well, I didn't think. I don't know. I thought you just wanted this to be a casual thing between us, so when I knew I was in love with you, I was afraid to let myself believe you could love me too."

"Amy," he whispered and released her arms as he kissed her softly, and she wrapped her arms around him. "How could I not love you? You're everything I've ever wanted. I loved Stacie, I love her still, but what I felt for her wasn't anything close to what I feel for you. She was my first love and will always be a special memory for me. She was my past, but you're my present and my future. I know your first marriage wasn't great, but I promise this one will be."

"M-m-marriage? You didn't say anything about marriage, Zach."

"Yes, I did."

"Nooo," she said very slowly, dragging the word out. "You asked me to move in with you—you didn't say anything about marrying me."

Zach let out an exasperated breath. "Do you think I'd ask you to move in with me without marrying you first?"

Amy searched his eyes and saw he was serious. "You don't know much about asking a girl to marry you then, do you?"

"What was wrong with that?"

"Crap, Ellison, you don't just say you want someone to move in with you and assume they know it means love and marriage, too. Lots of people move in together without ever getting married. It's *not* the same thing."

Zach sat up on the edge of the bed, swallowed the last of his champagne. "I didn't know that," he said and stood.

"Where are you going?"

"I'll be right back, just relax."

Amy piled pillows behind her and punched them up. She blew a puff of air. She hadn't meant to hurt his feelings but he'd caught her off guard, and she hadn't been ready for that question. She hadn't even known he was in love with her, so how was she supposed to know he wanted to live with her? And marry her? *Men.*

When he came back into the bedroom he was fully clothed, wearing the suit he'd brought to wear when they'd planned on going out to dinner. She looked at him and had never seen a sexier man in her life. Desire curled through her and she swallowed hard.

"What are you all dressed up for? Are you leaving?"

"Come here," he said and held a hand out to her. She took it, slid across the bed and sat on the edge facing him. He bent down on one knee in front of her.

"Amy, I know we haven't known each other longer than a few months, and have only recently begun to get to really know each other, but I think I fell in love with you the first time you came barging into my office."

He chuckled at the look she gave him. "I

know I wanted you the first time I saw you. I'm a simple man, you've seen how I live, and I don't really need much, but I need you. And I love you with all my heart and soul. I'll never hurt you, Amy, I promise. I'll always be faithful and there will never be anyone for me but you. I will give you everything I'm capable of giving and I'll take care of you all my life. If you'll let me," he added and grinned. "I want you to move in with me for the rest of our lives and I bought you this to prove it." He opened the lid of the little black box he'd been holding and handed it to her.

Her mouth fell open and her hand shook as she took the box from him. He reached for her and shut her mouth with one finger under her chin.

"Zach," she whispered. She looked at the diamond ring and then at him. "This is an engagement ring."

"Is it?" He took the box from her, turned it around and looked at it. "Crap, I told them cuff links. Now what am I going to do?" He rolled his eyes, took the ring from the box and slipped it on her finger. "Amy, will you marry me?"

"Oh, Zach. Yes, yes. I will marry you." She flung her arms around him, her body slammed into his, toppling him over backward, and when they hit the floor, she kissed him all over his face.

He put a hand on each side of her face and drew her head back so he could look into her eyes. "I love you, Amy. Always believe that."

"I love you, too." She kissed him again.

"Good, now get up and let me take this monkey suit off. We have some celebrating to do."

~ Ten ~

They rode to work together in Zach's truck, kissing when Zach dropped Amy off at her building. Grinning from ear to ear as she entered the elevator and rode it up to her floor, she just couldn't quite believe Zach had asked her to marry him.

"Good morning," Samantha said as Amy walked into the D.A.'s office.

Amy couldn't stop grinning as she told Sam, "Come into my office." She was as giddy as a sixteen-year-old girl on her first date.

Samantha followed her into the private office and shut the door. "What has gotten into you, Amy?"

Amy held out her left hand. "Look."

Sam took Amy's hand. "Oh my God, Amy." She looked into Amy's eyes, then back at the ring. "How? When? *Who*?"

"Zach Ellison. Last night. On bended knee." Amy grinned even wider at the look on Samantha's face.

"You've *got* to be kidding? You and Zach? When? How? You never even said anything."

"It's all been so fast. I don't know. All we did was argue every time we saw each other and then we started having lunch together. And the other night when you didn't show up for dinner, I ran into Zach at the restaurant and we had dinner and I went home with him. Then I took the next day off..."

"I knew it."

"We spent the whole day together riding horses and..." Amy giggled. "Well, we spent the whole day and night together and then we met at my house last night and, well, he proposed."

"*Oh. My. Goodness,*" Samantha said in stunned surprise. "He sure works fast, doesn't he? He's never even looked at another woman around here, then you go out to dinner and he proposes. Well, shave my head and paint my butt blue!"

Amy burst out laughing. "Sam!"

Sam laughed, too. "No one else heard that. I am so happy for you, Amy. Really. Congratulations." The two women hugged, and Sam asked, "Have you set a date yet?"

"No, not yet. It's so sudden we haven't had time to even discuss a date, but I want you to be my maid of honor when we do, okay?"

"Oh Amy, you're going to make me cry." Sam wiped a tear and they hugged again.

The phone on Amy's desk began to ring. "Let's have lunch, okay?" she asked Samantha as she reached for the phone.

"Okay, I'll see you then." Sam shut the door as she left the office.

"Amy Logan," she said into the phone.

"Can you get down to my office?" Zach asked.

"Sure. When?"

"As soon as possible." He hung up.

Amy looked at the phone and set it in the cradle. Now *that* was the detective she knew and loved. Picking up her brief case, she stopped by Sam's office to tell her where she'd be, and Sam raised her eyebrows and grinned.

"It's business," Amy called out as she pushed the main doors open, and heard Samantha laughing as she went.

Amy could see Zach through the glass in his office door. He was bent over the papers on his desk with a pencil in one hand, the other massaging his temple. She went in without knocking. "Hey, what's up?" She smiled as she shut the door.

He looked up and grinned. "I missed you."

Shaking her head, she told him, "That better not be the only reason you called me down here, Ellison." But she was smiling when she sat down in her usual chair. "Besides you saw me less than an hour ago."

"I know, but I wanted to see you again."

"Zach, you can't just call me down here because you want to see me."

"Why not?"

She laughed. "Because I have a boss who will fire me, that's why."

"Then I guess I better make this an official visit. Look at this," he said, handing her a piece of paper.

Amy looked it over and her eyes went wide. "You found her?"

"It looks that way. Want to go to California with me?"

She looked up from the sheet in her hand. "I don't know if I can get the time off."

"It'll be company time. I'll call Stanley." Picking up the phone, he dialed the number, and it didn't take long before Amy's calendar had been cleared for the next week.

"How did you do that? That old goat never gives an inch. And why will it take a week?"

"I've known Stanley since he was an

assistant D.A. himself and there was the little matter of his arrest that I managed to smooth over..."

"Wait, wait, wait. His arrest? *Stanley was arrested*? I've never heard a word about that."

"Of course not, and no one else has either. It's just between me and good ol' Stanley. I'll tell you about it later. And it's going to take a week because I want it to take a week."

"That's a misuse of taxpayer dollars, Detective. I don't think I can allow that. I am an officer of the court, you know."

Zach rolled his eyes and rubbed his head. "The first two days are on the state—that's for business—and the next five are on me. I just got Stanley to give you the time so we can take a detour to Cancun, get married and have a short little honeymoon. Look woman, are you always going to be this difficult to surprise?"

Amy was speechless, but only for a few moments. "You want to take me to Mexico and get married?"

"Only if you want to, darlin'. If you don't want to get married, we don't get married. We can just spend a few days in Mexico together."

"Oh, Zach." Amy sniffled. "You are the sweetest man I have ever known."

"Is that a yes?"

Amy nodded. "It's a yes. Oh, no, I told Samantha this morning that you proposed and I asked her to be my maid of honor."

"Look, darlin', if you want a church wedding with all that other stuff, then that's what you'll have. I don't care, I just want you married to me."

"That's all I want, too, Zach. Sam will understand. When do we leave?"

"The plane leaves at seven-thirty this evening. I'll drop you by your place first, and while you pack, I'll run over to my house and throw a few things together. And don't forget to pack a bikini. I plan on seeing you in it a lot." He grinned that charming lop-sided grin of his. "And out of it a lot more," he added.

~ * ~

The plane taxied down the runway and then lifted off. Amy watched the airport grow smaller as they ascended into the sky. She'd had lunch with Sam and explained she and Zach were eloping to Mexico. Sam was so happy for them both she cried again and didn't even mind that she wouldn't be able to attend the wedding.

Landing at the airport in Oakland, they retrieved their luggage from baggage claim and went to the rental car desk. Within an hour they were headed south on Highway 101 to Salinas where they hoped they'd get some good information from Abigail Johnson. Checking into their hotel first, they planned to go to Abigail's first thing the next morning and then be in Cancun by that afternoon.

~ * ~

Zach knocked on the door of the single-family home. "This is Detective Ellison with the northern district of New Mexico." He waited a few moments and then knocked again. Finally, a female voice asked who it was and Zach held up his badge to the peephole.

The door cracked open. "What do you want?" the woman asked.

"I want to ask you a few questions about Clarence Broom and Mark Abernathy, ma'am."

"Who? I don't know anyone by those names."

"Are you Abigail Johnson?"

"Johnson is my maiden name, it's been Rignotti for the past sixteen years."

"Would it be all right if we came in and asked you a few questions, showed you some pictures?"

She opened the door and invited them in. A petite woman in her early forties, she was slim and pretty and invited them to sit. Zach knew right away that a woman of her size couldn't have murdered the two men on her own—she simply didn't have the weight behind her.

As they sat on the sofa together, Amy sat quietly in the chair across from them, and Zach handed Abigail two full-face photographs, one of Broom and the other of Abernathy. "You don't recognize either of these men?"

She stared at both pictures for a long moment, then handed back the one of Abernathy. "I've no idea who that one is, but this one—" She waved the picture of Broom. "—used to live with my sister."

Zach took the picture from her. "Your sister? What is her name?"

"Eileen," Abby said as she rose from her seat, walked to the dining room and opened a drawer of the buffet. She returned with a photo album and opened it, and showed him a picture of a young girl about twenty years old with long blonde hair.

"She was a mixed up girl. She started

running away from home when she was about thirteen and our parents brought her back time after time, but she just ran away again. And again and again. She got into drugs, went from man to man, and we hardly ever heard from her.

"Then sometime in the mid-eighties she called out of the blue one day and announced she'd met Clarence, moved in with him and was expecting a baby. She sounded as if her life was on track. She sounded happy and so excited about having that baby. I thought maybe she was finally going to be all right. About four months later we got a call from the police telling us she was in the hospital. Clarence had beaten her so badly she'd gone into labor early and the baby didn't make it." Abigail paused for a moment and wiped the tears from her face with the back of her hand. She took a deep breath, blew it out and continued.

"I drove down to Bakersfield and got her, and brought her back home with me. She was so depressed she didn't eat, didn't get out of bed. I was worried about her and took her to a doctor. He gave her some pills and said she'd get over it. About a week later, she was gone. I didn't hear from her again for nearly two years." Abigail inhaled a calming breath before continuing.

"The police called again, said Eileen had been raped and stabbed and left for dead. I went back to Bakersfield and got her. I didn't even recognize her when I showed up at the hospital. She was beaten so badly, and stabbed numerous times. She didn't even look like herself, and eventually had to have plastic surgery to repair her jaw. Again, I brought her home with me, but as soon as she was able to leave, she did, and I've never heard from her again. I thought maybe she'd finally been killed, or killed herself.

"By then I had been dating David and about a year or so after Eileen left, he and I got married. Life goes on, you know? I've got a twelve-year-old son and a ten-year-old daughter that have never known their aunt. Sometimes I still get angry with her for that, and because I lost my sister as well."

Abigail drew a tissue from the Kleenex box and wiped her nose. "Did you come to tell me she's dead?"

"No," Zach said with a shake of his head. "Clarence Broom was found dead several months ago in New Mexico. The other one is Mark Abernathy, and he's also dead. He's the one who raped and stabbed your sister. We wanted to question her about them since she's the only common link we've been able to find.

"Do you know why your name came up instead of hers?" Amy asked.

"I don't know." Abigail shrugged. "She used my name from time to time when she'd get into trouble with her creditors, but it wouldn't have been too difficult for her to use my name and get I.D. She'd be able to get my birth certificate, social security number, or whatever else she needed."

Zach nodded. He hadn't been hopeful when he knocked on Abigail's door but now he had a picture of his only suspect. Abigail and Eileen looked quite a bit alike, he thought as he looked at the picture again. Abby didn't have any information that would help in locating Eileen

Johnson—if she was still alive—so he obtained as much information on Eileen from Abby as he could and promised to return the picture as soon as he had it copied.

Eileen had only been nineteen when the picture was taken so Zach would have it computer aged when he got back to the office, and hopefully get a better idea of what the woman he was looking for would look like now. After thanking Abigail, he and Amy said good-bye.

~ * ~

"Wow," Amy said when they were back in the car. "That was something. Is your job always like this?"

Zach laughed. "Sometimes, but mostly it's a lot of paperwork, just like yours."

"Do you think Eileen is alive?"

"I hope so since she's the only clue we have. She may have changed her name and moved away, too."

"Even then, wouldn't you stay in touch with your family? I can't imagine not having any contact with my family for nearly twenty years."

"It happens more often than you think. I've picked up bodies that when I found their families they hadn't heard from them in twenty years or longer. It's a lot more common for the homeless and mentally ill, but she might be mentally ill, given the trauma she's been through."

"Maybe I can get her off on an insanity plea," Amy said.

"Sweetheart, you're the prosecutor—it's not your job to get her off."

"You know what I mean. Maybe Rick will take her case *pro bono*."

"I don't think you can prosecute this case, Amy. I think this is a conflict of interest for you. You're getting too close to this case and empathizing with the person we think is the perp."

She looked at him and then turned toward the window and stared out. He reached for her and lifted her hand to his mouth.

"Don't pout."

She turned to him. "I do not pout."

"Then scoot yourself over here so I can touch you," he said and pulled her to him.

"Look, let's just forget about this entire case and think about the week we'll have together in Mexico. Sound like a plan?"

Amy nodded and managed a smile for him. "Yes, a good plan."

~ Eleven ~

The weather in Cancun was balmy, bright and sunny. They took a cab from the airport to their hotel and checked in. Amy squealed when Zach opened the door to their room. The opposite wall had a sliding glass door with floor-length windows on either side that gave them a wide-angle view of their private beach. The door slid open to a veranda decorated with white wicker furniture and potted plants. The room itself was large with a sitting area also decorated with white wicker furniture with cushions covered in white, with blue accent pillows. The king sized bed was covered with a pretty white lace bedspread printed with tiny blue flowers and blue pillows of all sizes and shapes. The dresser and bed tables were dark brown and highly polished teak wood with pretty clear crystal lamps with blue shades.

Amy spun in a circle in the middle of the room, "Oh Zach, it's wonderful."

"It is pretty impressive, isn't it?" He set down their luggage and picked up his fiancée. She wrapped her arms and legs around him and pressed her lips to his.

"Thank you," she said breathlessly. "I couldn't have dreamed of anything better."

"Are you sure you don't want to wait to get married back home in a church with our friends and family present?"

"No." She shook her head. "I want to marry you right here."

"Good, because I all ready made arrange-ments for the ceremony."

He set her back on her feet and took her by the hand, leading her through the sliding glass door onto the deck. Spread out before them was a beach of brilliantly white sand that ran into brilliantly blue water that seemed to go on forever. "We're going to have a sunset ceremony right there on the beach—if that's all right with you?"

She nodded and wiped a tear from her cheek. "I don't know what to say, Zach. How did you arrange all of this so quickly?"

"Lots of cash," he said dryly and then quickly laughed. "It wasn't difficult. They apparently do a lot of this kind of stuff down here."

She threw her arms around him and kissed him passionately.

"Now don't start something I have no intention of finishing," he said as he caressed her face. "The next time I make love, it will be with my wife." Amy started crying then. "Baby," he held her close, "what's wrong?"

"Nothing's wrong. I'm just so happy."

Zach shook his head. "*Women,*" he whispered, and hugged and kissed her softly. "Come on, I'm starving. There's a restaurant right here in the hotel."

"Let me fix my make-up and change my clothes first," she said, and disappeared into the bathroom and Zach heard another squeal.

~ * ~

Amy stood in the middle of her dream bathroom. It was at least half the size of the outer room. The walls and floors were made of shiny, white marble with blue veins. The double sinks were shaped like large clam shells sitting on a marble counter and the mirror behind it went to the ceiling. There were two toilets on the wall next to the sink and a wall with another door that faced her next to the toilets.

She went to the door and turned the brass handle. It opened into a room of the same blue-veined marble with a large Jacuzzi tub in the middle of the floor, with potted plants lining the walls on either side and stacked on little tables of varying heights in the corners to give the effect of sitting in a pool in the jungle. On the back wall and two sidewalls were showerheads at different levels, with a rain shower in the ceiling.

Amy took a deep breath and called to Zach. "Baby, you've got to see this bathroom."

He came into the room and stood beside her. "Wow, this is cool." He began stripping out of his clothes.

"I thought you were hungry?" She grinned at him.

"It can wait." He kissed her and started taking off her clothes.

"Wait a minute, buster. You just told me the next time we made love, we'd be married."

"We're just taking a shower," he whispered and kissed her again.

"Uh-uh." She pushed him away. "I like the idea and I'm making you stick to it. So if you want a shower, you're taking it by yourself."

"You're no fun."

"I will be after we're married," she said mischievously, squeezing his arm as she shut the door to the Jaccuzzi.

Amy smiled when she heard the water

come on. "I hope that's *cold* water," she shouted, but knew he couldn't hear her.

She couldn't find faucets for the clamshell sink and was puzzled by that. She looked under them, felt around them, and then noticed the little white button barely discernable from the marble wall and pushed it. A little square piece of plastic set into the marble slid back revealing a small rectangle shaped hole and water began pouring out of the wall and into the clamshell. Amy was delighted and squealed again. By the time Zach had finished his shower, she had changed her clothes, fixed her make-up and was ready to go.

~ * ~

They entered the open-air restaurant and were immediately seated at a window table so they could see the ocean and watch as people strolled along the beach hand-in-hand. Zach ordered a pitcher of Margaritas and told the waiter they'd like to wait a little while before ordering dinner. A few minutes later, the waiter set the drinks, glasses, and a platter of *hors d'oeuvres* on the table.

"I thought you were hungry," Amy said.

"I am, but we're in no rush. Besides I have something for you," he said with a wink.

"I don't know what else it could possibly be. You've given me everything I could ever ask for. More than I would ever ask for. I love you so much, Zach."

He took her hand, kissed it, and then said, "I love you, Amy. Look behind you, darlin'."

She turned slowly and found her parents and brother behind her. Jumping to her feet, she shrieked, "Oh!"

Looking from her family to Zach, she found herself wrapped in her family's arms. She just couldn't believe the man she was about to marry had actually been able to arrange all of this on such short notice. Zach introduced himself to her father, Tom, and shook hands with him and her brother, Chris. Her mother, Anne, refused a handshake and instead hugged him. The waiter pulled another small table close to the one where Zach and Amy were sitting and brought up extra chairs. Amy sat next to Zach with her family sitting across from them.

"I just can't believe this," Amy cried, still wiping her eyes with her napkin. "Lot of good it does for me to wear make-up when it seems to run down my face more often than not lately."

They ate, talked and laughed, and drank for the next two hours, then it was time to get ready for the wedding ceremony. Amy's mother accompanied the couple back to their room so she could help her daughter dress and Zach could get his clothing and dress in one of the rooms he'd arranged for Amy's family.

"What do you think?" Amy looked expectantly at her mother when Zach had gone.

"I think you're very lucky, and you look very happy," her mother answered with a hug, and they were both crying again.

"I can't believe he did all of this. To bring you all here like this when I didn't even think I'd have a chance to tell you about it until it was over. He is the most wonderful man I've ever known."

"I think so, too. And I can tell your father

likes him as well. Although we were so surprised when he called. We had no idea you were even seeing anyone."

"I wasn't, well, not really anyway. I just can't explain it. We work together, sort of, and we didn't even seem to like each other. He irritated me all of the time. I thought more about murdering him than I ever did of dating him."

Her mother laughed. "That's exactly how I still feel about your father. Now let's get you ready. Where
is your dress?"

Amy unzipped the hanging bag. "Zach doesn't even know I bought it, but yesterday when Sam and I went to lunch we did a little wedding dress shopping. I know it's not exactly a wedding dress, but since we're getting married here, I wanted something I could wear later. I can wear it with no shoes now that I know we're getting married on the beach. But I want you to see it on me first, okay, Mom?"

Her mother dabbed another tear and Amy ran into the bathroom and showered quickly. Then she shaved her legs, brushed her teeth, and slathered flower scented cream all over her body. She slipped the dress over her head and wiggled it down her body, smoothing it and turning side to side in the mirror. It was absolutely perfect. She opened the bathroom door and stepped into the room where her mother waited.

"Amy, you are beautiful," her mother exclaimed. "The dress is perfect."

Amy twirled for her mother. The white dress had thin spaghetti straps and scooped modestly in front, and the straps criss-crossed down her back. The thin material was almost sheer enough to see through, but not quite because the soft under layer draped against her skin and the sheer outer layer floated around her. The dress hung below her knees, with the back draping halfway down her calves.

"You'll take his breath away," her mother said. "Let me put your hair up. I'll let some of it fall around your face so it'll give you a soft look, and the rest I can pin up so it doesn't look too styled, but it'll be beautiful."

"Here." Amy handed her mother an over-sized barrette made from mother-of-pearl. "I bought this when I bought the dress. I didn't know if I would use it or not, but I think it will go with the dress, don't you?"

"I think it's perfect."

Amy sat on a stool while her mother fixed her hair, then stood in front of the mirror and carefully applied her make-up. When she was finished, she stood before the full-length mirror and turned slowly around. She couldn't believe she was looking at herself in the mirror, and she couldn't believe she was just moments away from becoming Mrs. Zachariah Ellison.

Just then there was a knock on the door and her mother opened it to let her father in. He held both of Amy's hands and looked her over. "You're beautiful, doll," he said as he kissed her cheek. "And it's time to get you out to the beach."

Her mother kissed her and hurried out the sliding glass door to join her son, Zach, and the minister at the water's edge. Amy looked out at them—everyone was barefoot and the men's pant legs were rolled up above their ankles. Taking a deep breath, she exhaled slowly.

"Ready?" her father asked.

"Yes," she said with a brilliant smile. "No. Daddy, I don't have flowers. I forgot all about them, I was so busy trying to find the dress."

Her father went to the door and opened it, stepped back in and presented her a bouquet made with Bird of Paradise flowers.

"Oh, Daddy. Thank you." She hugged him tightly.

"You're welcome, but it was your mother's idea." He opened the sliding glass door, offered his arm and escorted his only daughter down the veranda steps and across the beach to stand beside Zach before the minister.

~ * ~

Zach's heart pounded in his chest. He'd never seen anyone more beautiful than Amy was as she walked slowly across the sand holding her father's arm with one hand and the bouquet of flowers clutched in the other. He had never felt love like this before, had never known he was capable of feeling anything this deeply, this completely. Never a man to weep, he felt tears welling up in his eyes now and blinked hard to fight them back. She did this to him—made him feel things he'd never thought himself capable of. She made him feel possessive, obsessive, made him feel protective and very, very male. He took a deep breath and smiled at her, then held out his hand and she took it.

They beamed at one another and, with joined hands, turned toward the minister, who cleared his throat and began reciting the vows. When Zach kissed his bride, the family applauded. Then everyone kissed everyone else.

"Hey, squirt," her brother said and hugged her.

"Respect your elders," she said as she punched him.

"You might be older, but I'm bigger," he declared and lifted her off her feet, then kissed her on the mouth, making much noise while doing so.

"That's my wife you've got your mouth on there, Sonny." Zach said with a mock frown.

"Then you can have her," Chris said and literally tossed Amy into Zach's waiting arms.

"Come on, family," Zach said as he set Amy on her feet. "We've got some serious celebrating to do."

The celebration went on all night. They drank and danced and then moved to other clubs and bars until Amy was sure they'd been in every nightclub in Cancun and had been congratulated by every local and tourist alike. When dawn came, her parents finally gave in and went to their room. Shortly after, when the sun began to rise, Amy's brother also decided to head back to his room, although he did have a long-legged *senorita* on his arm when he went. When Chris winked as he left the club, Zach and Amy both laughed.

"Finally." Zach pulled Amy against him. "I thought they'd never leave."

"What did you have in mind?" She stood on her tiptoes and kissed him.

"A champagne breakfast."

"Seriously?"

"Absolutely. Come on."

He took her by the hand and as they went through the lobby of their hotel, Zach stopped at the desk and told the clerk to have a full champagne breakfast sent up an hour later. Amy giggled. She was exhausted and a little bit drunk, but she was also happier than she'd ever been in her life. Following Zach as he led her by the hand to their room, she stood by as he put the key in the door, pushed it open and scooped her up in his arms.

"I have to carry you across the threshold, Mrs. Ellison," he said and then kissed her as he carried her into the room and kicked the door shut behind him.

Laying her on the bed, Zach knelt on the floor before her, then lowered his head and rested it on her lap, while Amy curled her fingers in his hair and stroked his cheek. He looked up at her, wrapped his arms around her waist and drew her close to him.

"Amy, I want you to know I love you. I love you now and I will love you forever. You are what I have always wanted, and have dreamed of having. And I tell you this now so that in the future, when all the new wears off and you're thinking of killing me, maybe you'll remember how much I love you and not be too hard on me.

"I know I'm going to make you angry, and I'm going to work late, and I'm going to forget to bring you flowers, and I won't feel like having sex sometimes, and when all of that happens, will you promise you'll just think about right now and remember how much I love you?"

Amy giggled through her tears, and sniffled when she said, "Zach that was almost the most beautiful thing I've ever heard. But I promise I'll always remember how much you love me. And I figure I can live with late nights and no flowers if you can live with PMS and lost cases. Deal?"

Zach shook his head. "Nope, you're the only one who has to put up with crap. I expect *you* to be perfect." He looked at her seriously.

She smacked him upside the back of his head. "It looks like the honeymoon is over before it's even begun."

He grinned that lopsided grin that always made butterflies come to life in her stomach, and she lowered her head to his and bit his bottom lip. Grabbing her by both arms, he jumped up, throwing her backwards onto the bed, then landed on top of her.

Much later, they lay curled into each other's arms when room service knocked on the door. Zach groaned, wrapped a towel around his waist, and rose to open the door. Amy dove deep under the covers, her face red as the young man pushing the cart into the room glanced at her and smiled. Zach grinned and handed him a few dollars before shutting the door behind him.

Setting the trays on the bed, Zach rejoined Amy on the bed, and both sat facing each other with legs crossed and fed each other strawberries and melons, followed by champagne. After they had demolished the ham and eggs, bagels and cream cheese, and a variety of pastries, they fell into an exhausted sleep.

~ Twelve ~

The applause was loud when Zach returned to work on Monday morning. Only Ellen had known Zach and Amy had actually gotten married, and she'd been only too happy to pass along the information. There were balloons in his office, and a variety of gifts had been left on his desk. Grinning as he looked over everything, he then moved it all to a place on the bookshelf.

"Zach, do you have a minute?" Ellen asked as she came into his office.

"Of course," he replied cheerily.

Ellen raised her brow. "Congratulations, Zach. We're all very happy for you and Amy, although a lot of us are very surprised as well. You're good at keeping secrets."

He merely looked at her.

"We were all wondering if you were planning on having a reception. We kind of feel like family around here you know, and with you two running off and getting married in Mexico, we all feel like we've been left out. Anyway, Frank and I would like to host a reception for you if that'd be all right? Just something out at the house, nothing fancy. Would you mind?"

Zach rose from his seat behind the desk and walked around to where she stood. Ellen took a small step backwards. Zach grinned. "Come here." He pulled her into a tight embrace and told her, "Amy and I both appreciate that, Ellen. Thank you for thinking of us."

She blushed slightly. "If I'd known that all it took was a little party to get a hug out of you, I'd have done it a long time ago."

"Just let me know all the details, okay? Or better yet, why don't you and Amy go to lunch one day and discuss it?"

"That sounds like a good idea. I'll give her a call."

"Good. Now get back to work," he said as sternly as he knew how.

She turned, a smile curving her lips, and went back to her desk, shutting his office door softly behind her.

Zach pulled the paper work from his briefcase, along with the picture of Eileen Johnson. He stared at her for a moment, tried to imagine what he would do if he'd been in her shoes, if he'd been beaten, raped, stabbed, left for dead, and had a baby die because of it. He shook his head—he knew what he'd do. He'd kill somebody.

With the picture in hand, Zach headed for the lab. Sue Jamison, one member of the forensic team who had worked the scene, was there and he handed it to her.

"I need this photo aged about fifteen years," he told her. "The girl may actually look a little older than an average person would since she used drugs and had the crap beaten out of her more than once."

"Rode hard and put up wet, huh?" Sue looked at the picture.

Zach nodded. "Probably more than once. She's also had a little plastic surgery done because of a broken jaw and broken nose. We're trying to locate the surgeon who worked on her to see if there are any pictures of her in the medical records. For now though, this is all there is."

"Come on, this shouldn't take too long if you don't have some place to be." As he followed her, she continued, "Heard you tied the knot last week. Congratulations."

"Thanks," he said and smiled. It was a small world and news traveled fast.

"Okay," she said as she sat on a stool in front of a computer. Opening the scanner, she laid the picture face down, pushed a button and scanned it into the computer. The picture then came up on the screen and Sue began typing, then took the mouse, clicked it a few times and a new picture came up. It was the same girl, just a little older looking. "What do you think?"

"Can you age it a little more?"

"Sure."

"And change her hair, maybe shorten it, change the color or something."

"No problem." Sue moved the mouse over the screen and the face aged a little more. The new picture came up with an older woman who had shorter, darker hair. Sue made multiple prints on the screen with different jaw lines and different noses. She changed the hair color and its length, added some weight to the face, and then ran them one by one on the slideshow. Zach thought they all looked pretty good since he didn't have any idea what Eileen Johnson would look like now, but the pictures Sue had created gave him something to work with and one of them was bound to be close. Sue printed a copy of each picture for him, and handed the original back.

"Hope that helps," she said.

"Yeah, me too. Thanks, Jamison, I appreciate it."

"No problem, just name your first born after me," she said and laughed.

"A boy named Sue? Sounds like a country song to me." Zach pushed open the double doors and could still hear her laughter when he pushed the button for the elevator.

Riding the elevator up to his floor, he went into his office, sat at his desk, and picked up the phone, then put it down again. He was thinking about what Sue Jamison had said—his first-born. He hadn't thought about having kids since he and Stacie had tried, but since Sue had mentioned it, he was sure thinking about it now. He hadn't even brought it up to Amy, hadn't once asked her what she wanted in that area. But then, she hadn't brought it up either. Maybe she didn't want to have children, and if that was the case, then he didn't have anything to worry about. Did he?

He hadn't used a condom with her. She hadn't asked him to either, but then it was almost common knowledge that he hadn't slept with anyone since Stacie. Amy hadn't slept with anyone in over two years, so neither of them had been worried about disease, but he hadn't even considered pregnancy. She must use some sort of birth control, he thought but then again, why would she when she wasn't having sex with anyone?

"Great, Ellison." Tapping a pencil against the ink blotter on his desk, he blew out a breath. He'd been so busy falling in love with her he hadn't even paid attention to some of the most basic things. It wasn't that he didn't want a baby with Amy, because he did, but he wanted *her* more than anything else, and he just wasn't willing to risk it.

He'd wanted a child when he'd been married to Stacie, but in the trying she'd gotten cancer and died. In his head he knew the two were in no way related, the doctors had even told him so, but in his heart, he wasn't so sure. Maybe trying to get her pregnant for so long had caused the cancer to start developing, maybe it was his fault after all. He wasn't taking the chance with Amy.

Taking another breath, he blew it out, then got back to work. He sent the pictures of Eileen Johnson over the inter-office mail to have them distributed to every law enforcement agency in the country. Listing Eileen Johnson as a missing person ensured her bio would be matched against active missing persons' reports, as well as with unidentified bodies around the country. He had to find Eileen Johnson. He knew she was connected to the two murders, and he was more certain since speaking with her sister than he had been before. She also reminded him of someone, but he couldn't place who it was. He tapped the pencil some more, though he couldn't concentrate on Eileen Johnson just now because he had the situation with Amy on his brain.

He picked up the phone again and dialed. "Amy, we're going to lunch, meet me in the lobby," he said when she answered and then he hung up just as quickly.

~ * ~

Amy looked at the receiver and shook her

head. The man definitely needed to work on his phone manners. Glancing at her watch, she saw that it was just after ten and she had paperwork to catch up on. Actually, she had a *lot* of paperwork to catch up on. Her week in the sun with Zach had been great for her tan, but it left work piling up at the office and she'd be playing catch up for the next two weeks. She shuffled through the cases she needed to deal with first, the upcoming arraignments and trials she couldn't delegate, and then looked through the new cases that had been assigned to her. She worked through the next two hours and it was Zach's impatient voice on the other end of the phone when she answered it just after noon to remind her she was already ten minutes late for lunch.

"I'm sorry," she said and kissed him when she got off the elevator in the lobby. "I've got such a backlog of work, I lost track of time. How are you?"

"I got the computer-aged photos of Eileen Johnson distributed all over the country. I put her out as a missing and endangered person, hoping I'll get a hit faster. That's only if she's in the system, and that's a big if. Unless she's dead of course. Did you pick up that new case—what was it, Newcomb?"

She shook her head as they slid into a booth at a diner a couple of blocks from the where they worked. "Not that one, but I got enough of the others. I don't need another murder right now.

"Thanks, but I don't need a menu," she told the waitress. "Just bring me water with lemon and the Reuben with no dressing."

"Burger and fries and an iced tea," Zach ordered. He looked out the window and then back at Amy.

"What's the matter with you, Zach? Is everything all right?"

He reached across the table and took both her hands in his. "I guess we should have talked about this before, but it never really crossed my mind until today."

"What is it? You're making me nervous."

"We never talked about having kids, Amy. I never even thought about birth control with you."

Amy looked at him, realizing she hadn't really thought about it either, and there hadn't really been time to with everything happening as fast as it did. She could tell by the look on his face this wasn't going to be something she wanted to hear. "And you don't want children with me, right?"

"It's not a matter of not wanting children with you—it's a matter of not wanting children at all. And since you didn't bring it up, I just presumed you didn't want them either. I'm an idiot for not thinking of it, but after what happened with Stacie, it's just not a good idea."

She pulled her hands out of his, let the waitress set their lunch on the table and forced a smile as she said thank you. "I see," she said quietly after the waitress had walked away.

"I just don't want to be responsible for that, Amy. Do you understand?"

Oh, she understood all right. He didn't want the responsibility of a baby and her as well.

Fine, she could live with that. She'd been happy with her career and there really wasn't time for a baby in their lives anyway, so if that's how he wanted it, she didn't have a problem with it.

"I understand," she said and sipped her water.

"You don't know what a relief that is," he said with a smile as he bit into his hamburger. "Aren't you going to eat?" he asked through the bite.

"I think I'll get a go box and take it back to the office with me. Work has really piled up, you know." She sat staring out the window.

"By the way, Ellen and her husband want to throw a little reception for us out at their place. I told her to call you for lunch and the two of you can work on the plans together."

Amy forced a smile. "Fine, that'll be fine."

"Are you all right, Amy?"

"Sure. I just have a lot of work to get back to. I'm playing catch up," she said and forced another smile as she looked at him.

Zach took the last bite of his burger and washed it down with tea. He shoved some French fries in his mouth and threw some money on the table. "Okay, let's go."

His mind was at ease now that he knew for sure Amy felt the same way he did about not having kids. It would kill him if anything happened to her, and if not having a baby was a sacrifice he had to make to keep her safe, then he would willingly make it. It had been hard enough losing Stacie that way and he would not go through it again. Amy was the single most important thing in his life, and it didn't matter what he had to do, or sacrifice, as long as she stayed safe. She was the only thing that mattered to him.

Amy got off the elevator, went into her office and shut the door. She set the to-go box on her desk and paced around the room.

"Oh, just go along with him, Amy," she said aloud. "Don't even try to tell him what you want, just tell yourself you don't have a problem with it. Don't have a problem with it—like I don't have a problem with it. Of course I have a problem with it!"

Sitting down, she shuffled papers for a while but didn't even see what she was looking at. This was definitely something they should have discussed. She had been so overwhelmed with everything else it hadn't even occurred to her that he wouldn't want children with her. She wanted children, she always had. She just hadn't thought she'd ever be with someone she could have them with. And Zach surely fit the bill for father material. Oh, but wouldn't they make beautiful children together? Lots of dark-haired boys, and lots of sweet, blue-eyed girls. She wanted lots of kids with Zach. He just didn't want any with her, she thought sadly, then wiped the tears from her face and settled down to work.

"Hey," Sam said as she opened the door and looked at Amy. "What's going on?"

"Nothing," Amy lied and waved her in. "Just all this work piled up and I'm not in the mood to deal with it."

"I can help you," Sam offered.

"You have enough of your own work, Sam, but I appreciate the offer."

Sam handed her an envelope. "Zach had this sent up for you."

Amy opened it to find the computer aged pictures of Eileen Johnson. She looked at each one carefully, then looked up at Sam and grinned. "Our suspect looks a little bit like you," she said and handed one of the pictures to Sam.

Sam looked at it and frowned. "You think so? I don't see it. Who is it anyway?"

"Oh, a woman connected to the Broom and Abernathy cases. Her name is Eileen Johnson, but she's apparently fallen off the face of the earth." Amy took another file out and spread it on her desk.

"I've got to get back to work," Sam said and hurried out of Amy's office.

Amy looked up and started to call after her friend and ask Sam what was wrong, but her phone rang. "Hello, Amy Logan."

"Hi Amy, it's Ellen, how are you?"

"I'm drowning under a pile of work, but other than that I'm good. How are you?"

Ellen laughed. "That's to be expected. Zach said he mentioned the reception to you at lunch today. What do you think? We could get together tomorrow over lunch and discuss the plans. Does that work for you?"

"That will be great, Ellen. And I want you to know we both really appreciate you going to the trouble."

"It's no trouble at all. We're just happy to be able to do it for Zach and for you too, Amy."

"Thank you, Ellen. See you tomorrow." She hung up the phone and picked up the pictures of Eileen Johnson.

She really does resemble Sam if you look at it just right, Amy thought.

She sighed and put the pictures in the envelope and placed it in the desk drawer, and went back to the pile of folders on her desk.

~ * ~

Two weeks later Zach and Amy were the center of attention at a reception being held at Frank and Ellen Goode's home south of the city. The Goodes' had bought the house years ago before their boys had been born and the drive into town had been a long one. But now the town had come to them. They were both grateful they'd bought the thirty acres surrounding the house just two years after moving into the house, since it was the only thing that had saved them from encroaching neighborhoods as the area around Albuquerque had grown by leaps and bounds.

The backyard had glowing lanterns strung around the deck, leading down the steps and along the path to the pool. Torches had been set around the perimeter of the yard and candles had been set on the tables. Fresh flowers in vases stood between the candles on the tables and more candles floated on lily pads in the pool. Tables laden with food had been set up buffet style and the gas grill sizzled with steaks, hamburgers and hotdogs. Another table had been arranged with buckets of ice, an open bar, and plenty of soft drinks for the kids and non-drink-ers.

The entire police department had shown up, along with the lab and coroner's office and the district attorney's office. They had come with their spouses, children, significant others, or by themselves, and everyone came bearing gifts. The table had been draped with a paper tablecloth and was now buried under the mountain of gifts deposited there. Next to it was a table decorated with flowers and candles and in the center was a beautiful three-tiered wedding cake.

Amy had been hugged and kissed so much she thought her face must be covered with as much lipstick as her mouth, if there was even any lipstick left on her mouth at all. She wore the dress she had when they'd married in Cancun and Zach was wearing the same slacks and shirt, but this time they both wore shoes. They had started out standing side-by-side, but somewhere along the way, he'd disappeared and she was left to deal with the well-wishers alone. She would make sure he paid for that one later.

Finally, everyone had arrived and began settling into groups. The chatter was a chaotic buzz that rose above the music being piped from the stereo in the house. Ellen found Amy sitting in a chair alone and brought her a glass of champagne.

"No thanks, I'm not drinking tonight."

"Are you feeling all right?"

"Sure, just a little overwhelmed. I didn't expect this many people to show up."

"I'd like to say it's because they all love Zach, but it's mostly because they'll take any excuse at all to get drunk for free."

Amy laughed and blinked when the photographer flashed in her face again. "If he takes one more picture of me tonight, I'm throwing him in the pool."

"You need to mingle, get to know everyone," Ellen said with a laugh and patted her leg before moving off into the crowd.

Amy stood and searched the crowd until she finally caught sight of Zach with a group of men, a beer in one hand and a cigar in the other. She smiled and tried to make her way toward him. The past two weeks had been extremely busy for her as she got caught up on her cases and started on new ones, and though she had wanted to talk to Zach some more about having children, the time never seemed right. She sighed and smiled as one more person hugged her. That's when the first wave of nausea hit her. It had happened a few times over the last day or two, but she didn't pay it any mind since she didn't have a fever or any other symptoms of the flu. She just thought it was from all she had going on both at work and at home. But this time, she didn't think it would just be the queasiness she'd had before.

Hurrying toward the house, she barely made it into the bathroom before she began throwing up. She hated vomiting, it made her feel so weak and out of control. Leaning heavily over the sink, she ran the water and splashed some over her face and rinsed out her mouth. She looked at herself in the mirror and smoothed her hair, then opened the door and stepped into the hall to find Ellen waiting for her.

"Are you ill?" Ellen asked.

"No," Amy said with a shake of her head. "I guess it's just all the excitement."

"Come with me," Ellen ordered, taking her by the hand and leading her into the master bedroom. "Sit down," she said and patted the bed beside her. Amy sat. "You're pregnant aren't you?"

Amy sighed and nodded. "I think so. I haven't gone to the doctor yet. I was hoping it was just the flu or something, but then I realized my period is nearly two weeks late."

"And you haven't told Zach either, have you?"

"No, and I'm not going to."

"That's not exactly something he won't notice eventually," Ellen commented with a laugh.

"I know. I just don't know what to say to him. He doesn't want children."

"What? Why would you think that? I know Zach and he wants kids."

"He told me he doesn't the same day we got back to work when we came home from Mexico. He told me how he wanted kids with Stacie and now he doesn't want the responsibility. But we hadn't even discussed kids before we got married, it all happened so fast. I wasn't on the pill because I hadn't had sex in two years, and he never mentioned anything about it either. Then when he told me he didn't want kids, I just went along with it and never told him I do want kids." She sighed. "And I probably got pregnant the first time we had sex."

"I think there's been some miscommunication along the way here. And I also think you need to talk to Zach."

"Not tonight. And please, Ellen, don't say anything to him."

Ellen put an arm around her and squeezed. "I won't say anything. Believe me there's nothing sweeter than being able to see the look on your man's face when you tell him he's going to be a father. I wouldn't let you miss that for the world. Now let's go back out and get you something to eat."

Amy nodded and followed Ellen back to the party.

Amy made it through the rest of the night with no more queasiness, and by the time it was over, she was glad since Zach was in no condition to drive them home. Frank and his two sons loaded the pile of gifts into the back of the Avalanche and Amy waved good-bye as she backed out of the driveway. Zach was already snoring with his head against the passenger window.

When they pulled into the driveway Amy had to shake Zach a few times to get him awake enough that she could help him into the house. He was trying to kiss her and fondle her breasts while she tried getting his boots and clothes off of him. Laughing as she swatted his hands away, she finally managed to get him into bed, then undressed and slid in beside him. He slung an arm possessively around her and began snoring again.

~ * ~

Samantha Jane Waters had made her way through the guests until she'd found Amy and Zach standing side by side. She'd hugged them both, wished them well, and apologized because she couldn't stay longer. She'd left the party and gone home, where she'd spent some time pacing, trying to figure out what to do. Eventually she'd gone to bed and fallen asleep.

The nightmare wasn't the same as usual, this one was about Zach and he was chasing her.

She ran and ran until she was out of breath and could run no more. She was frantic now, struggling through blackness, unable to find her way. Close to panic now, she could hear Zach calling her name. "Eileen, I know who you are. Eileen. Eileen." He kept calling her name over and over. It was a name she hadn't heard in over fifteen years, yet he knew it was hers.

Fighting her way through the darkness, she couldn't outrun him. And then she was in an empty room, sitting in a chair and Zach was pacing around her. Then Amy was there, pointing a finger at her, accusing her, telling her she was going to prison for the rest of her life. And Zach was grinning, but it wasn't Zach's face, it was Mark Abernathy's face and he was coming toward her. He grabbed her by the throat and began choking her. She tried to fight, but she couldn't, so she looked at Amy, tried to plead with her for help. But Amy just looked at her and shook her head. "You're getting what you deserve, Eileen. You only got what you deserved."

Sam sat up, fighting the darkness, gasping for air until she realized where she was. She turned on the bedside lamp and covered her face with her hands. Then she threw back the bed covers, slipped her feet into her fuzzy house slippers and went into the bathroom. She looked at herself in the mirror and washed her face.

Heading into the kitchen she looked at the clock on the stove. It was four in the morning. Sam took a deep breath and made a pot of coffee. When it was done, she poured a cup and took a sip. The dream was slipping away, but she couldn't shake the sense of dread or the fear it had left behind.

~ Thirteen ~

What *was* that noise? Zach's head felt like it was going to come off and now there was that incessant ringing. Why didn't Amy answer the phone?

He felt across the mattress to Amy's side of the bed and found it empty. He groaned and reached for the phone on the nightstand.

"What?" His voice was gravelly and there was sand in his eyeballs.

"I hate calling you on a Sunday, Zach, but we've got another body, and I didn't think you'd want me to wait until Monday," Ron said.

"Crap." Zach didn't want to spend the day at a crime scene, especially since he was barely even sober and felt like he was two steps from dying. "All right, but it's going to take me bit to get going. I'll call you back when I'm up. Tell everybody to relax."

Zach fumbled a bit as he tried to put the phone back on the cradle. Of all the days for him to be called in to work, he thought as he scrubbed his face with both hands and tried to focus, but it hurt too much. And he still didn't know where Amy had gone.

Sitting up very slowly as his head pounded like twelve demons were trying to get out, he swore under his breath and had to stop halfway up because his stomach began to lurch. Oh this was going to be a peachy day. He finally got himself to a sitting position and was truly dreading being on his feet, but he forced himself to stand and held a wall for support. After a few seconds he began to steady and made his way into the bathroom and turned the taps on in the shower. Standing under the hot water for a long time, he finally began to feel at least a little human again.

He dried off and stumbled into the kitchen and found a fresh pot of coffee made, but Amy was still nowhere to be found. *Where are the aspirins? Anything for this headache.* He rummageed around in the cupboards until he found some Alka-Seltzer. He grimaced as he swallowed the bubbling water, and then noticed Amy was watching him.

"You're awake. I expected you to be in bed until late."

He squinted to bring her into focus. "I might be upright, but I don't think I'm awake yet. My head is aching and I haven't decided if I'm going to puke or not. What time is it?"

"After eleven."

"Crap. Where did you get off to?"

"I fed the animals and wrestled with Earl."

He hugged her. "You didn't have to take care of the animals. I'd have done it later."

"They needed feeding, so I fed them. It wasn't a big deal. What are you doing up?"

"Ron called—there's been another murder, so I've got to get out to the scene. You want to come?"

"Really?"

"Sure, it won't hurt you to see it firsthand. And with the way I'm feeling, you can drive."

~ * ~

Ron met Zach at the truck as they pulled up next to a police cruiser, and he nodded to Amy. "You look a little rough," Ron said with a laugh.

"Thanks." Zach ran a hand through his hair.

"Zach, this one is pretty bad, you might want Amy to stay in the truck."

"It's up to you babe. Just remember how it went when you saw the autopsy on Abernathy."

Amy nodded. "No, I want to see it." She got out of the truck slowly and followed Zach to where the body had been found.

Zach tilted his head, clasped his hands behind his back, and began walking a slow circle around the body. It was definitely done by the same person, but Zach's stomach wasn't handling the scene at all. This was definitely not the day to be walking a crime scene like this one. The heat was nearly unbearable, and between that and the hangover, he was feeling more than just a little green around the gills.

Zach surveyed the body and shook his head as he slowly circled it. It was tied spread eagle just like the last two had been, but this time the body was in a kind of sitting position and the muzzle of a shot gun had been situated to be balanced between the victim's rearend and the ground.

And it had gone off. There was a string looped around the trigger of the gun that had been tied to a tent stake in the ground behind it. When the position of the shotgun changed, it put tension on the string and the tension caused the trigger to depress.

From the way the victim was hung from the trees, and because of the injuries he'd sustained prior to the gun going off, he wouldn't have been able to stand erect for long. As he slumped forward, he had caused the gun to fire. Zach shook his head and made another trip around the body.

The exit hole at the sternum was about eight or ten inches across. Guts had been blown completely out of the body and the ground was littered with pieces for at least twenty feet to the front. What was left of the lungs was hanging out, and muscles and skin were hanging down from the ragged hole the blast had left. The eyeballs were bulging from their sockets and body fluids had been forced up the throat and out the mouth, nose, and ears. The smell of feces, burnt flesh, and blood mixed with the smell of gunpowder hung relentlessly on the air.

~ * ~

Amy turned and ran back to the pickup. It was so hot out and after seeing the crime scene, her stomach revolted. She hung on to the tailgate and vomited, continuing to retch long after her stomach was empty.

"Here, I brought you some water," Ron said, coming up to her.

Amy hated anyone seeing her throw up and tried to wave him away, but he wouldn't go.

"Don't worry about it, you aren't the only one who threw up over this one," he said to her as she used the water to rinse her mouth. "About five of the guys lost it earlier. This one was pretty bad."

"Thanks," she said and handed the bottle back to Ron. "I think I'll sit in the truck and wait for Zach there." She smiled weakly when Ron opened the door for her. "Thanks." She got inside the vehicle, started the engine, and turned the air conditioning on high, then leaned back in the seat and shut her eyes.

Feeling better in the cool air, she was glad she at least had an excuse for being sick. And luckily, Zach hadn't noticed. She knew the time would come when he would notice, and she knew she had to tell him soon. But she didn't know how she was going to do it. Afraid of his reaction, she worried what he would say, worried he might ask her to do something she would have to say no to, something that might cause a rift between them that couldn't be remedied. She felt a flicker of panic within her. No, she refused to believe they wouldn't somehow work it out. They had to because she loved him and she knew he loved her too. It just had to work out.

Zach opened the truck door and climbed in. He looked at Amy. "Are you okay?"

"Yeah, just a little queasy. That was pretty gruesome."

"It was for me, too. Sorry I made you come along."

"No, that's okay. You ready to go home?"

"Yeah, the autopsy will wait until Monday and I need to lie down. Not feeling so good myself right now."

Amy put the vehicle in reverse and pulled slowly away from the scene. "That's because you drank an entire keg of beer by yourself."

"Don't remind me," he groaned.

"Let's go home and go back to bed. I think I could use a nap myself."

~ * ~

On Monday morning, Zach went downstairs with Ron as Pete prepared to autopsy the body that had come in on Sunday. Zach and Ron wore paper aprons, face shields and gloves. Pete was wearing scrubs covered with a rubber apron, along with a face shield and gloves. The three men stood and stared at the body. It was such a gruesome, unbelievable sight, and none of them had seen anything like it. This even beat out Abernathy's gruesome demise. But there would be some useable evidence this time. They had the shotgun.

Pete looked at the two men. "Well, I think I've determined the cause of death," he said dryly.

Ron looked green, and Zach managed a groan. "Can we just get this over with?"

"Cops have no sense of humor," Pete said and shook his head as he turned on the camera and recorder. "There isn't a lot left inside of him and what is there is mush. Half of the heart is missing, and the lungs are mangled. I honestly have never seen a body in a condition as bad as this one. I'm going to start with the brain."

~ * ~

Zach sat at his desk with Ron in the chair across from him. Ron said, "At least we didn't have any trouble getting an I.D. on him. He's also got a record out of California."

"Yeah." Zach nodded. "We need to find out if he knew a woman named Eileen Johnson, or Abigail Johnson. Find his family, if he has any, and get some information. I want to know if he knew her. Besides being in prison in California and winding up dead in New Mexico, Eileen

Johnson is our only other commonality with the other two victims."

"We're still waiting to hear from ballistics, but I doubt there were any fingerprints on the gun. However, it came from somewhere and we'll find out what we can."

"Get over to the lab and talk to Sue Jamison, see what she says and get back to me."

Ron left the room and Zach picked up the file. The victim's name was Alan Thomas. He was fifty-nine years old and had served both state and federal time dating back to the late seventies. He'd been arrested on numerous weapon charges, drug charges, and bank robbery, along with a myriad of other lesser charges.

Zach sighed. At least Eileen Johnson was consistent and only killed bad guys. How a girl as pretty as Eileen had gotten so messed up that she found herself involved with the likes of Clarence Broom and Alan Thomas was beyond him. He couldn't blame her for Mark Abernathy, however, since she'd been his victim. At least that's the way it looked, but maybe she had been his girl-friend, or perhaps she'd dated him. Zach didn't have those answers, but when he finally caught up with her, he was going to ask.

~ * ~

Amy and Samantha sat at a table having lunch together. "You didn't stay long at the party," Amy said as she poured ranch dressing over her chef's salad.

"I know, there were just so many people there, I was getting claustrophobic."

"I understand that. I swear, I got lost in the crowd and that stupid photographer kept flashing in my face and if I had to smile at one more person and say thank you, I thought I'd scream."

"I shouldn't have left you alone. I should have taken you with me."

Amy laughed. "I think I would've gone."

"Have you learned any more about that woman Zach is looking for?"

"Not yet, but with this last body, there was evidence and Zach is certain it will lead to her."

"Evidence? Really?"

"Yeah, Zach seems to think so but I haven't heard what it is yet. Of course, they haven't finished at the lab or autopsy, so Zach probably won't have anything definitive for weeks yet. But he's hopeful this time they'll break the case. He's been on edge over all of this, frustrated over not getting anywhere. I'll be glad when it's all wrapped up and we can live in peace."

"So nothing has really changed then?"

"No, not really."

The conversation turned to more mundane things like upcoming cases and shopping. The hour went quickly by and the two women walked back to the office.

~ * ~

Zach looked at the fax Ellen had just brought him. He finally had something on Eileen Johnson.

"Ellen, get me a flight to Bakersfield," he barked into the phone, pushed a button for another line, and dialed Amy's number. When she answered, he said, "Sweetheart, I have to go to

Bakersfield. I finally got something on Eileen Johnson. I'm leaving on the next flight out, but I'll be home tomorrow afternoon.

"I wish you could go with me but I understand your schedule. Yeah, yeah, I love you, too." He grinned when she said she loved him, then hung up.

~ * ~

Zach grabbed a taxi after landing in Bakersfield, California and headed to the police department. He introduced himself to the woman at the window, showed his badge and signed in. He was ushered into the inner offices and shown to Captain Bernhard's office.

"Detective Ellison, it's a pleasure meeting you. I'm Glen Bernhard. Please, have a seat."

The two men shook hands, and Zach glanced over the man, his round belly, bald head, and handlebar mustache, all putting Zach at ease. "Nice to meet you. Call me Zach."

"Okay, Zach. I understand we have some information you need? I've had the records pulled up from the archives. We didn't go real high tech around here until the mid-nineties, so a lot of stuff from the seventies and eighties didn't make it into the computers and were stored in the basement, uh, archives." He chuckled and picked up the phone. "Nancy, see if Richard's got all the info on Eileen Johnson up here yet." Then he replaced the phone.

Zach settled into a chair. "We appreciate your help in this matter. We've had three male bodies show up over the past eight months without a bit of evidence. All we've had to go on is a common name, Eileen Johnson. She was the first one's girlfriend and a victim of the second one, and we don't know about our most recent one yet. We just got him on Sunday, so we haven't gotten very far. We've had Eileen's name out on the wire as a missing person for about three weeks now and you're the first response we got."

Bernhard nodded. "Yeah, and we wouldn't have picked her up except she was arrested with Broom once. That was the only reason she was even in our system at all, but after we dug through the paper records, we found a few more things on her." He looked up as the office door opened.

A pretty woman with shoulder length, brown hair and big brown eyes, who Zach guessed to be about thirty years old, walked into the office with a file folder in hand.

"Here's the file you wanted, Captain," she said with a smile.

"Nancy, this is Detective Ellison out of New Mexico. Detective, my secretary, Nancy."

Zach stood and offered his hand. "Nice to meet you, Nancy."

"You too, Detective. I hope you have a nice visit while you're here."

"Thanks." He watched her as she left the room.

Bernhard flipped the file open and glanced at it. He handed Zach a sheet of paper. "This is the arrest record from when she was hauled in with Broom. It was originally a traffic stop, but he had meth on him, and Eileen was with him, so she got hauled in, too. We questioned her and I think she was more afraid of him than of us. We let her go after a few hours. Broom bonded and got ten days in jail over the dope." He shook his head. "Of course, that was back before crank really carried any stiff penalties. He'd have gone to prison for it if we'd had the laws then that we do now."

"She had good reason to be afraid of him from what I hear," Zach commented as he read over the report.

Bernhard passed the rest of the records to Zach. "Yeah, she got a raw deal with him, but as you'll see, she wasn't the only one. He had numerous complaints filed against him by the women he lived with. He beat the daylights out of each of them on numerous occasions, but none of them ever testified against him. He had them so afraid of him they believed he could even reach them from prison."

Zach was silent as he flipped through the pages. There were seven complaints filed against Broom in addition to the one for assaulting Eileen Johnson. Only two had resulted in arrest and Eileen herself had paid the bond. There was one report of Broom jumping bond and being arrested in Las Vegas with Eileen by his side. He didn't know what to make of it. She had so many chances to see him imprisoned for a long period of time, had chances to get away from him, make a new life for herself, and she hadn't taken it.

Zach simply couldn't fathom what would make a woman stay with a man like that when there were alternatives. She could have testified against him or she could have gone to a halfway house. She could have stayed with her sister, Abigail—he knew that for sure. It made no sense to him and that was another thing he was going to ask Eileen Johnson about when they finally met face-to-face.

~ * ~

Driving slowly down the driveway to his house, Zach saw Amy's little blue car parked near the back door. Iit made him smile to think of her in his house with her things there as well. She would be waiting for him, he knew, and supper would be waiting. He was amazed with her. Working all day just like she did, but also insisting on cooking for the two of them when they got home. He had tried to get her to stop and pick up something from a restaurant or fast food place but she always refused.

Pulling the Avalanche to a stop beside Amy's car, he hopped out. Earl was nowhere to be found and Zach figured the dog must be out with the cattle or had found himself a cool spot in the shade somewhere.

He walked into the house and from the laundry room could hear Amy in the kitchen chattering to someone. He walked softly to the doorway and peeked around the corner and almost laughed out loud. Amy was standing at the counter mixing something in a bowl, and Earl was sitting attentively at her feet looking up as she explained every step of the process to him. Earl had one ear up and one down, with his head cocked to one side as if he understood everything she was saying.

"Is Earl going to be cooking our dinner from now on?"

Amy screamed and jumped, throwing flour everywhere. "Zach! You scared the crap out of me. What are you doing sneaking up on me?"

Zach laughed out loud. "That's some watchdog you've got there, he didn't even know I was in the house. I could've been a dangerous burglar or something."

She tipped her head up to take the kiss he offered her. "He knew it was you, that's why he didn't bark. If you'd been a danger to me, he would've ripped your throat out."

Zach laughed. "Sure he would." He gathered her close and kissed her again. "What's for dinner?"

"I'm making biscuits and I've got some chicken frying over there. As soon as I get these in the oven, I'll make mashed potatoes, and I'll make some gravy off the chicken grease."

"Are you trying to make me fat, woman?"

"I don't want you wasting away," she said with a grin.

"Not much chance of that. I'm going to get a shower."

Amy finished cooking their dinner while Zach showered and dressed. They sat at the kitchen table together while they ate and Zach told her what he found out from Captain Bernhard.

"I feel so sorry for her, Zach."

"She had chances to leave, to get away from him for good, and she didn't do it."

"It's not always as simple as that, Zach. Sometimes women do things that don't make sense to anyone else."

"You can say that again," he said with a laugh.

"That's not what I meant and you know it.

Look, it's like when I was married to Andrew and I thought he was having an affair, but I didn't say anything to him."

"Why didn't you?"

"Because we were married and marriage is based on trust. If I had said something to him, accused him of cheating, it would be saying I didn't trust him."

"And you shouldn't have trusted him because he *was* cheating."

"That's not the point. What if I asked you if you were having an affair? What would you say?"

"I'd say that's ridiculous. I'd never cheat on you."

"You wouldn't, no, but Andrew was cheating, and if I had said anything he would have denied it and said I was the one at fault. Men like that, the ones who lie and cheat, and the ones who hit women always make it the woman's fault. Eileen couldn't fight back because every time she did, it made it worse for her. And I doubt he was the first one to ever hurt her. She was probably abused by her father, or someone else, when she was growing up. She was probably also sexually abused when she was young." Amy shook her head.

"You can't use what you know about life to determine what she should have done in that situation. Besides, you're a good man—you have no idea what bad men do to women like Eileen."

"And you do?"

"Yes, I do."

He raised an eyebrow and looked at her.

"I was originally going to be a psych major

before I decided on law, so for one semester I volunteered at a shelter for abused women and their children. It's part of the reason I changed to law. I thought I could be more useful prosecuting the kind of men who use and abuse women and children."

He looked at her for a moment then wiped his hands and face on a napkin and leaned toward her. "Kiss me," he said softly. "You're too good, you know that?"

She kissed him and giggled. "So are you. Now finish your dinner. I made chocolate cake for dessert."

"I don't want cake for dessert," he said with a wink.

"Hmm, how about ice cream then?"

He shook his head.

"Cookies?"

"Just you."

~ * ~

Much later, after the dishes were done and they had made love, Amy stared into the darkness listening to Zach's soft snoring. She'd come so close to telling him about the baby while she'd been lying on his chest in the warm afterglow of their lovemaking. She wanted to so badly, but she was also afraid of his reaction. She loved him so much, was so happy she was pregnant, and so confused over what to do about it.

Yes, she understood what a man could do to a woman; how he could cause her to feel she should take the whole of responsibility for the things that happened in their relationship. She turned onto her side facing away from him and he rolled over, wrapping an arm around her, and he held her tight against him. A tear slid down her cheek and it was a long time before she fell asleep.

~ Fourteen ~

"Zach, you're not going to believe this." Ron came into the office.

"Tell me what you got, Ron."

"Alan Thomas was married to Eileen Johnson."

"Seriously?" he said as he reached for the paper Ron was holding. He read it over twice and then sat back in his chair. "It has to be more than just coincidence. She has to be the one doing this."

"It looks that way, but I just can't figure a woman doing murders like this. They're so cold-blooded, so messy. It just doesn't sit right with me, Zach. What kind of maniac is she?"

Zach looked up at Ron. "The kind that's been treated like crap by every man she ever knew. Amy gave me an idea last night, so I called the sister, Abigail, this morning, and asked her about their father, how he treated them, and such.

"He was a drunk and beat their mother, as well as both sisters. She told me Eileen had been molested by two of her uncles, one was her mother's brother and the other her father's brother. And when she finally had the guts to say something to her folks, guess what mommy did? She backhanded her, and told her she must've liked it or she wouldn't have kept it a secret. Her father refused to go to the police and said they'd never believe a kid over an adult.

"So, you see, the very people who should have been protecting her were actually protecting the ones that abused her. And they were abusing her as well, physically, verbally, and mentally. So the only kind of men she ever hooked up with was more just like them. It may have taken her a while, but I think Eileen's intentions are very clear. She's not just exacting justice—she's getting a little closure."

Ron looked at his hands. "Sorry, guess I spoke out of turn."

"Yeah, but I'll forgive you this time. Now let's just find the woman, can we?"

"I've been going through motor vehicle records in California and the surrounding states, but I haven't found anything at all. Not all states have gone to thumb prints, or fingerprints, for driver's licenses, so I haven't gotten a hit there either. It seems as if she's just fallen off the face of the earth. We could be wrong, Zach, it might not be her. She might have died. That might be why we can't find her. She could be a Jane Doe somewhere and we'll never find her."

"I've thought of that too, but this is the only thing that makes sense. These murders are personal, very personal. She's telling us something, telling them something. She's telling them she's not taking their crap anymore, and she's telling us we didn't do our jobs, so she's doing it for us."

"Why here? Why not in California? It doesn't make sense to me."

"Because I think she lives here," Zach said simply.

Ron looked at him. "You think she lives here in Albuquerque?"

"Or near enough."

"How do we find her?"

"Concentrate on drivers' licenses here, and check for her sister's name as well. She's used Abigail's name before. Talk to anyone who has the same vitals, check their social security numbers, and get work histories on them. Maybe we'll get lucky."

~ * ~

Amy sat at her desk with Sam across from her, sharing a pizza for lunch. It was raining and they'd decided to order in. "Zach's got more information on Eileen Johnson," Amy said between bites.

"Really?" Sam looked at her, hoping her voice wouldn't give anything away.

"Yeah, he thinks he might even be close to catching her. He thinks she lives here in New Mexico. They're going over DMV records and every woman that matches her description will be questioned. It'll take a while, but they'll catch up with her eventually."

Sam took a bite of the pizza and looked out the window. "Yeah, they sure will."

Amy took another bite of pizza and looked at her watch. "Crap, why does the time go by so fast when we're eating lunch? I have a deposition this afternoon. Are you going to be there?"

"I think so," Sam said as she swallowed. "Cooper wants us both on this."

"Good, I need your help. So I'll meet you in the conference room at one, okay?"

"Sure thing," Sam agreed and left the room without finishing the piece of pizza she'd had in her hand.

Samantha went back to her desk but she couldn't concentrate. She was worried now—they were getting too close. All of her hard work was about to go down the drain, and she wasn't about to go to prison for any of the men she'd killed. She worked too hard, for too long, to get to where she was to let anyone get in her way now.

She'd met Alan Thomas while he was in prison of all places. Clarence Broom had gone to prison while they were living together and was serving his time at the facility in Soledad, California. Sam had come to visit him and met Alan in the visiting room. Clarence was forcing her to smuggle drugs into the prison and Alan was the man Clarence gave them to in exchange for Alan keeping him alive. Clarence had burned one of the Mexican gangs for a lot of crank money and Alan had intervened on Clarence's behalf. So Sam had begun bringing heroin in to him every time she came for a visit to pay off his debt. He promised her money over the deal but it never came.

Of course, Sam knew nothing about what had happened behind the prison walls, knew nothing about the deal made to save Clarence's life. But she was still very afraid of Clarence and he used it to his advantage. He had beaten her enough, had belittled her, had made her feel worthless and useless to the point that she truly feared he would kill her as he threatened to so many times before. Even from behind prison walls, she was afraid he could still hurt her, could have someone else do his dirty work for him. She believed him when he said he would hunt her down after he was released and kill her. So she did what he told her to do.

Then, during one particular visit she

refused to bring any more dope into the facility and Clarence had shoved her up against the wall in the back of the visiting room, using his strength and the fear he could see in her eyes to force her to comply. The guard on duty didn't seem to even notice until she started screaming and kicking Clarence, who then backhanded her hard across the face. That got the officer's attention and she was allowed to leave. She swore she'd never come back. She didn't know what had happened to her because she was still afraid of him, but thought perhaps even if he really could have someone else kill her for him, at least the torment would be over. She just didn't care anymore.

Clarence kept calling her and even though she refused to accept the collect calls, he continued to call several times during the day, even when she wouldn't answer the phone. It rang constantly until she unplugged it and left it that way. A few days later she received a letter from Alan asking her to accept a call from him. He said if she did he would make everything right. She didn't know him really, had seen him in the visiting room a few times, but she accepted the call when the phone rang at the designated time he'd specified in the letter. She listened to him talking to her, telling her what an idiot Clarence was and how she was right not to trust him, or to even be with him at all. But he was telling her the truth when he said if she didn't bring the rest of the dope inside, they would kill him. Alan promised he would make sure she got something out of it as well, and she agreed to carry the dope in one more time. This

time it was four grams of heroin and that would
be it.

She bought the dope and took it into the
prison during a busy Saturday visiting day when
they all knew it would be crowded and chaotic.
During the count, when all of the inmates had to
line up and give their names and prison numbers
to the officer at the desk, Clarence had told her
to go to the refreshment machines and pass the
dope to him there. Since the line wound around
in front of the machines the hand-off wouldn't be
noticed by the cameras watching the prisoners
and visitors alike.

She was standing at the snack machines as
she was told, but when Clarence instructed her
to pass it to him, Sam refused. He called her
names, but she stood her ground and told him the
only one she'd give it to was Alan. And that's
who got it. When she left the prison she told
Clarence it was over, she'd not be back and it
was the last time she saw him—at least it was the
last time she saw him until she'd killed him. She
didn't answer his phone calls or letters, either,
and then moved from the area. After everything
he'd put her through, she was finally through
with him. She was finally able to be rid of him.

A couple of weeks later she received a
letter from Alan forwarded from her old address.
She read it and he seemed very nice, but she
didn't answer it because she was through with
convicts. The following week she received another letter from Alan and he was very funny and
sweet, but she still didn't answer the letter. The
following week a third letter came. And two days
a later a fourth letter came. The fourth letter did

her in when he told her since they were going to be married, the least she could do was answer his letters.

When she had finally written him back, it led to a visit, and within the month they were married in a makeshift ceremony in the prison visiting room. She spent the next four years married to a man in prison and visited him every weekend. He also made good on his promise to make sure she received compensation for all the dope she had brought in to bail Clarence's sorry ass out of debt. She wished she had just let the Mexican gang he had stolen from kill him.

Whenever Alan sent her the handmade cards from prison there would be two or three one hundred dollar bills glued in between the sheets of paper, and she received the cards several times a month. He had actually sent her close to a thousand dollars the first month, and it happened every month after that as well. For people who didn't believe cash and dope floated around inside prisons, Sam had been convinced it did—the old-fashioned way. It had been proven to her first hand.

Four years later Alan paroled and came home to her, and she had run across the tarmac when his plane landed and had gotten into trouble by the airport authorities for being in an unauthorized area. She had thrown her arms and legs around him and kissed him for all she was worth and that night, back at her apartment, they'd made love for the first time.

But after nine years in prison, he didn't adjust as quickly as Sam thought he would, and of course, he had a hard time finding a job. He also had to appear for random drug testing and his parole officer dropped by whenever he felt like it. Completely unannounced. The parole officer was a nice enough man, but it all added up to a lot of pressure and stress that was also felt in their relationship.

When Alan began drinking, he was mean, and then one of the neighbors accused him of busting in her door and telling her he wanted to have sex with her. He, of course, denied it, and Sam had believed him, but somewhere in the back of her mind, there was that little niggling of doubt. And Alan had two children from a previous marriage and there was tension with his ex-wife and her parents. It just all seemed to pile up very quickly and then all hell broke loose.

He and Sam fought constantly and the fighting became physical, and then he began staying gone for days at a time. It had ended when he left her for a woman who attended the substance abuse classes he was mandated to also attend. Sam had invested five years of her life, and all of her time and energy into him, and another woman walked off with him. It was more than she could take.

She hadn't intended to kill him, hadn't even felt the need to really. What she had really wanted was to make it, to be something, and then to flaunt it in his face. She had emailed him from a library computer and told him how well she was doing, how much money she was making now, and wanted to know if they could get together for lunch sometime. Alan had moved to Denver, Colorado, where he managed a motorcycle repair shop, and she had driven all that way to see him.

Dressed in a very expensive business suit, with expensive pumps, and her nails and hair perfectly done, she knew he wouldn't recognize her. None of them had because of the plastic surgery that had been done, thanks to the scars and damage left by Mark Abernathy. She walked into the shop and spotted him immediately. His hair was still long, hanging past his shoulders, and his beard was still full, but it was all white now, and she thought he looked more like Santa Claus. She walked up to him and smiled. He asked if he could help her and she told him she needed a date for lunch. He had smiled quizzically and then she told him who she was. His chin had literally hit his chest.

They'd gone to lunch and spent the rest of the afternoon together. He was still married to the girl he'd left her for, but he said it didn't matter and he wanted to spend time with her— for old times' sake. She'd laughed and they had wound up in a motel together and had sex. He just hadn't cheated *on* her now, but had cheated *with* her and she snapped. She didn't know why or how, but she wound up back in Albuquerque with him dead asleep in her back seat, and she'd taken him out to the desert at gunpoint and killed him.

Well, she hadn't actually killed him. Not outright. She'd placed that single-shot 10-gauge shotgun up his butt and tied the trigger off so if he moved at all it would go off. She left him to deal with it himself. He may have found a way out of it, actually. There was the possibility he'd not die. It had been a slim possibility, but a possibility nonetheless. She told him to hold still, someone would eventually come along and help him or call the police. It appeared he'd chosen not to be still.

Sam knew they would catch up with her eventually even though she'd been careful not to leave any forensic evidence of her own. She hadn't even handled the shotgun or the shells without using gloves and she knew the gun couldn't be traced back to her since it had been stolen when she bought it. It might take months before they ever came to ask her questions, she thought, and there had to be thousands of women in the motor vehicle computers who would match her description in general. But she knew that eventually they would catch her.

Still there might be another way. She had to think about it, plan it just right, and maybe she'd walk away free and clear. Pacing around the living room, she ran it over and over in her head. It wouldn't be easy to pull off, but then no good plan was easy. She had money saved up— she'd had nothing else to do with it but save it. And she'd always wanted to live on an island, or the beaches of Mexico. But she wasn't going to just disappear—they'd still be looking for her that way. No, she had to be dead in order to get out of this alive and not wanted by the police. And she thought she had the way to do it.

~ Fifteen ~

Amy sat on the table in the examining room and waited for the doctor. She'd talked to the nurse and peed in a cup. She was having her first prenatal exam and wanted to hear the doctor tell her everything was fine with her and the baby.

The door opened and a nice looking older woman walked inside. "Hello, Amy. I'm Doctor Freeman. How are you today?"

"I'm good. A little nervous, but I feel pretty good."

"Is this your first pregnancy?" Amy nodded. "Any morning sickness?"

"A little, but it hasn't been too bad the past few mornings."

"No spotting or bleeding?" Amy shook her head. "Are your breasts tender?"

"No, I don't think so."

"Okay, you can lie back and I'll get a nurse in here," Doctor Freeman said as she stepped into the hallway and returned with the nurse who helped get Amy's feet positioned in the stirrups and prepared an instrument tray for the doctor. After a breast exam, a pap smear, and an internal exam, Amy was allowed to sit up.

"You appear to be in good health and so does the baby. I just wanted to re-check your information though—are you sure about the date of your last period?"

Amy nodded. "My periods are like clock-work and never vary more than a day either way, but I always mark my calendar because I get busy and forget the dates and don't want my period to start unexpectedly while I'm in court or something. Did you find something wrong?"

"No, no, nothing like that," the woman said with a smile. "Your uterus just feels a little large for eight weeks. I think we should do an ultrasound and see what it looks like in there. Okay with you?"

"Sure, but what does that mean?"

"It doesn't mean anything yet, so why don't we get the ultrasound first and then we'll talk about it?" Amy nodded again and the two women left the room. The nurse returned a few minutes later pushing a large machine into the room in front of her.

"Don't worry, this doesn't hurt a bit," the nurse said good-naturedly. "The doctor does several ultrasounds every day."

When Doctor Freeman returned to the room, she turned the monitor around so Amy could see it too, entered some information with the keyboard, and the nurse flipped the overhead light off. Explaining she was going to do an internal ultra sound with a wand covered with a condom she held in her hand, the doctor told Amy to bend her knees and inserted the instrument into her vagina. Doctor Freeman began looking at the screen, stopping periodically to take measurements with some of the keys, and other gadgets, on the machine.

"See Amy, here's the placenta, and this is your baby, and that little fluttering thing right there is the heart," the doctor explained and pointed.

Amy choked on her tears. "I didn't know I'd be able to see it today. It has a heart."

The doctor laughed. "Yes, it does, a very strong one. And see this right here?" Amy nodded. "That's your baby's brother or sister."

It took a moment for what the doctor was saying to fully register in Amy's mind. Her eyes grew wide as saucers and her mouth opened, then shut, and then opened again. "Oh my... Are you sure? It can't be possible. You can't be saying what I think you're saying."

"I know it's a lot for one day, but yes, you're having twins."

"Oh, my goodness. Oh, my goodness. This isn't possible. Is this possible? No, it's not possible. Is it?"

"From what I'm seeing, I'd say yes, not only is it possible, but it's already happened. Now you have some real news to share with your husband."

Amy's face paled. "He doesn't know I'm pregnant."

"You haven't told him?"

"No. It's complicated. We've only been married two months. I just didn't know how to tell him."

"He'll take it much better than you think and you better tell him soon. He's going to need the next seven months to prepare for the babies just like you are."

Amy nodded. "Okay," she said weakly.

"Don't look so worried, everything will turn out fine."

Amy drove back to the office and shut her office door, and then picked up the phone and punched in the numbers. "Ellen, it's Amy, are you busy? Can you come up with an excuse to

come to my office without Zach knowing? Good.
Yes, right now."

When Ellen knocked on Amy's office door a
few minutes later, she opened it immediately,
grabbed Ellen by the arm and practically jerked
her inside. Amy shut the door and turned the
lock.

"I was waiting for you."

"Amy, what's the matter, you look white
as a sheet?"

"I just came from my first pre-natal visit
to the doctor," she said, still gripping Ellen's
arm.

"Is everything all right?"

"Yes. No. Oh, I don't know."

"Amy, tell me what's going on—you're
making me nervous."

"They did an ultrasound and it's twins,"
she blurted out.

Ellen took a moment to process what she'd
just heard. "You and Zach are having twins? Oh,
Amy, how wonderful."

"How wonderful? I haven't even told Zach
I'm pregnant, and now I have to tell the man who
doesn't want kids that he's getting two of them."

"Young lady, you listen to me. Zach wants
children. I know he does. He just blames himself
for Stacie's cancer because they were trying to
get pregnant when she was diagnosed. I think he
probably sees it as a way to protect himself from
the thought of losing you.

"Now, don't look at me like that. I know
it's a ludicrous idea, but then Zach is a man who
has to be in control, has to be able to take care

of everyone and everything. And Zach is so in love with you, it would kill him to lose you. Just the thought of losing you is enough to make him irrational.

"I know Zach, and I knew him when he was married to Stacie, and as much as he loved her, it was nothing like what I see in him for you. He is absolutely head over heels in love with you, Amy, and I never thought to see him like that. Now, I want you to promise me when you go home tonight, you'll tell him he's going to be a father."

Amy nodded. "I'll tell him. But I'm scared to death."

"Then go out to dinner, tell him over candlelight and a chocolate soufflé, but tell him."

"I will. Thank you, Ellen. What would I do without you?"

"I'm sure you'd be just fine. I've got to get back or he'll be wondering if I'm out looking for a new boss."

Amy laughed. "Okay, I'll see you later," she said as Ellen left her office.

A few seconds later, Sam stuck her head in the door. "Amy, you got a second?"

"Sure, what's up?"

"Well," she began as she shut the door. "I was wondering if you were planning on renting your house now that you've moved into Zach's place."

"I hadn't really thought about it, I've had so much else going on."

"I was thinking if you wanted to, I'd like to rent it from you. I live way out of town and it's such an inconvenience to drive all that way back and forth to work, or if I just want to come in to eat at a restaurant or go shopping. I'd love to live in town."

"That's funny. We decided to live in Zach's house because we both want to be further from town." She paused for a moment. "Yeah, if you want to rent it from me, that'd be great."

"Thank you. That's just great. Do you have the time after work to take me by there? I've never been there, so I don't know where it is."

Amy chewed on her bottom lip. "Okay, I've got a few minutes after work today."

"Good, and we can go in my car. It'll help me remember where it is if I drive."

"Okay, I'll just go with you after work. Zach's been working late every day trying to locate Eileen Johnson, so he'll never miss me."

~ * ~

Amy didn't bother to call Zach and tell him she was taking Sam by to see the house because she knew she'd be back in time to ride home with him before he even knew she was gone. She put her files away, cleared off her desk, and when she opened the drawer, she picked up the envelope with Eileen Johnson's pictures in it. She drew one picture out of the envelope and looked at it. She wondered what it was that made Eileen snap after all these years. What had happened that made her start killing these men at this time? It had been so many years since the atrocities had happened to her—surely something horrible had happened to set her off. She took another look at the photo and still thought it resembled Samantha, and then she put it away.

A few minutes later, Amy and Sam cruised through the traffic as everyone was trying to get home and it took a little time to get to the house. The two women walked through the house. Sam said she loved it right off and wanted to rent it. With that agreed upon, they got back into Sam's car and began driving when Sam said she had to run by her own house first and would then get Amy back to the office in time to meet Zach. Amy had looked at her watch and decided it wouldn't take too much more of her time to go with Sam.

They drove the dusty road out to Sam's secluded house and pulled into the garage and the door automatically shut behind them.

"Come on in," Sam said.

They entered the house through the garage door and went into the kitchen.

"Have a seat." Sam motioned to a chair at the table. "I'll be right back."

Amy sat as Sam disappeared down the hallway. Amy looked around. The furnishings were modern and very southwest in design. The house was painted in sand, beige, and creams, and the furniture was the same colors, as well as the carpets and rugs. There were no photos of family on the walls, no indication of any personal mementoes anywhere Amy could see and she found that odd. But not everyone was as sentimental as she was, and not everyone was as big a pack rat either.

After a few minutes, when Sam hadn't returned, Amy called out to her. "Sam, I don't mean to rush you, but I really have to be getting back or Zach will be having fits."

Suddenly, Amy felt the smack on the back of her head but before what had happened could even register, she was lying on the floor, out like a light.

~ * ~

"I'm sorry to do this to you Amy," Sam said as she tied Amy's hands behind her back, tied a gag around her mouth and blindfolded her. Amy was much easier to carry than the men had been, and Sam took her into the garage, opened the trunk of her car, spread a blanket inside and put a pillow in with it, then hauled Amy up and into it. She made sure the pillow was adjusted under Amy's head where she'd felt the lump from the blow.

Sam started the engine, opened the garage door and backed out. She drove west for hours until she came to Flag Staff, Arizona, then turned south on Highway 17, and a few minutes later, she turned onto a small two-lane paved road and drove west into the mountains. When she reached the little cabin, she turned the car off and went up the steps, lifted the welcome mat where the spare key was kept and opened the door. Turning on a light, she went back to the car, opened the trunk, and helped Amy out. Awake and frightened, Amy was able to walk and went into the cabin with Sam.

Once inside, Sam helped Amy to a chair and took off the gag and blindfold.

"What the hell are you doing, Sam?" Amy demanded as soon as she could talk again. "Untie me and give me a phone."

"I'm sorry, Amy, truly I am. I wasn't trying to hurt you, but I need your help and this was the only way I was sure I could get it without Zach finding out."

"Are you insane? What do you think he's going to do when he can't find me? What do you think he'll do to you when he finds you? You'll go to prison, Sam."

"No, no, I won't. That's why I brought you here. You've got to listen to me."

"Look Sam, I need to use the bathroom really bad and I need something to drink. Please, you have to let me use the bathroom. I'm pregnant and I have to pee all the time."

"You're pregnant?" Sam asked in disbelief. "You never said anything."

"Because I haven't told Zach yet, but please, let me use the bathroom."

"Okay, I'll untie your hands in the bathroom, but I stay in there with you."

"I don't care, just let me pee."

Sam escorted Amy to the bathroom and stood blocking the door with a gun in her hand while Amy used the toilet, then retied her hands and led her back to the table and tied her to the chair.

"I don't even know where to start to explain this to you, but I'll try." Sam took a deep breath. "You remember the picture of Eileen Johnson you showed me and said she resembled me?" Amy nodded. "She didn't just resemble me, she was me."

"*What*?" Amy almost shouted. "What are you talking about, Samantha?"

"I am Eileen Johnson, or I was a long, long time ago. I worked very hard to get rid of her and I was so sure she was dead, but then... well, then things began happening, and apparently she's back. I am not going to prison for killing those sick sons of Satan, Amy. They didn't get anymore than what they deserved." She snorted. "Less than what they deserved. But I sent all three of them to hell with my face being the last one they saw before they went. And I hope it's as bad for them there as they made my life here."

"You, you... you killed Broom, Abernathy and Thomas? *You* did those horrible things to those men?"

"Those 'horrible' things as you call them were less than what they did to me, less than they deserved to get." Sam began pacing the floor, and then she disappeared down the hall and returned carrying a shoebox. When she turned it upside down, pictures flooded the table, and Sam began turning the pictures over, laying them in front of Amy.

"That's me at three years old when my father's thirty-nine year old brother began mo-lesting me." She flipped another picture over. "Me at five after he had spent two years trying to get inside of me and told me *I'd* be in trouble if I told anyone. Here I am at seven when my mother's youngest brother started molesting me and making me do things no little girl should ever have to do. Oh, and that's me at eleven when I finally told my mother about my dad's brother and she backhanded me and said I must've liked it. And here I am at sixteen when I tried to kill myself the first time. And here at seventeen when I drank all the time to make the monsters go away and—"

"Stop!" Amy screamed. "Sam, that's

enough. Stop. I get it, okay? I get it." Amy's voice softened.

Sam looked at Amy, tears welling in her eyes. "I don't know what kind of childhood you had, Amy, but mine, well, I didn't really have one. My innocence was gone at three. And that SOB died of cancer and no one ever held him accountable. My mother's brother died also, with no one ever holding him accountable. It wasn't right. And when it came to it, I wasn't going to let them die without being held accountable either."

"Sam, what about Abernathy? He went to jail for what he did to you."

Sam laughed bitterly. "Oh, yeah, he went to prison for five whole years for raping me, beating me beyond recognition, and stabbing me, then wrapping a plastic bag around my head to suffocate me. I've spent more than fifteen years trying to deal with it, trying to get my life together, and he spent five, *five*, years in prison. Yeah, that was justice, wasn't it?" She pounded her fist against the table. "That wasn't justice, but what happened to him out there in the desert was."

"Sam," Amy said softly. "We know what happened to you with those men and we know what they did to you. They also did it to other women. You weren't the only one. And I agree, so does Zach. It's no great loss they're gone, but you still can't just kill them. I promise you, Sam, if you take me back, tell Zach what happened, we'll do everything we can to make sure you don't spend your life in prison. I don't see how you can even be prosecuted since we could plead out on insanity."

Sam looked at Amy and shook her head. "And I know you'd really try, Amy, but I'd go to prison for the rest of my life at the very least." She shook her head and played with one of the pictures on the table. "I have another plan. I'm going to die right here in this house and you're going to be my witness."

~ Sixteen ~

"Where is she?" Zach bellowed.

"Zach, you are not helping by throwing a fit." Ron tried to calm him.

"Look, she's gone and no one has any idea where she is. She wouldn't have just gone off without telling me she was going somewhere," Zach told Bill Ness, who was taking the missing persons report.

"You know we don't even do these for twenty-four hours," Bill said. "If it was anyone else, we'd be telling you to go home."

"I don't give a rat's long tail what you'd tell somebody else. I want every cop in this city out looking for my wife. Now!"

"Zach!" Ron bellowed over Zach's voice. "If you don't knock it off, we'll never get anything done. You're really not helping like this."

Zach grabbed his jacket without a word, although everyone in the room could read everything he was thinking by the look on his face.

"Wait a minute, Zach, I'll go with you." Ron shook his head and looked at Bill. "If you need anything else, you can access Amy's active files over at the D.A.'s office. I'm going to go make sure King Kong there doesn't kill anybody."

Zach and Ron headed for the elevator. Ron glared at Zach.

"Zachariah, your temper isn't going to do Amy any good. You've got to start treating this like a case and quit acting like it's your wife."

"She's my wife and she's gone. Don't you

get it?"

"Of course I do, but you're going to feel like a big idiotwhen you find out she's off with one of her friends 'cause you were working late and she didn't want to bother you by calling to tell you where she'd be."

"No, you're wrong. This isn't just a matter of her going out with one of her friends. My gut is telling me something is very, very wrong and I've got to find her."

"Where are you going?"

"I'm meeting Stanley at Amy's office. I'm going to search her desk."

~ * ~

With his friend on his heels, Zach went to Amy's office. There, he went through every case file she had but didn't find anything that would give him an idea of where she might have gone. He sat back in the chair behind her desk and opened the drawers. He found the envelope with the pictures of Eileen Johnson, and turned it over in his hand.

"What's that?" Stanley asked.

Zach held it up. "It's the pictures of our suspect." He took one of the photos out of the envelope. "She's the woman we've been looking for in the Broom murder."

"Mind if I look at that?"

Zach shrugged and handed the photographs to Stanley.

After studying the pictures for a moment, Stanley said, "If you gave her red hair and kind of softened up her face, she'd look like Sam."

Zach slowly turned to face Stan. "Let me see that." He looked at the face and knew Stan was right. He had thought she reminded him of someone from the first time he saw the picture, and now he knew it was definitely Samantha. Could she be the one they were looking for all along? Sitting right there under their noses the entire time?

"What's Sam's phone number?"

Stan recited it from memory and Zach dialed the phone. When her machine answered, Zach hung up.

"What do we have on Samantha Jane Waters, Ron?"

"Nothing that I know of," he replied.

"So get something."

"I can't believe Sam could be involved in anything illegal, especially not with Amy's disappearance. Not only is Sam one of our top prosecutors, she and Amy are good friends, Zach. Sam would never do anything to hurt Amy. You know Ellen was over here today too, maybe Amy said something to her."

Zach picked up the phone and dialed Ellen's number. "This is Zach and I need you to get over to the D.A.'s office right now." He hung up without giving her a chance to answer.

~ * ~

Zach paced the outer office, and that's where Ellen, and her husband, Frank, found him. They hurried down the hall toward him. Frank pushed the double doors open.

"What is it Zach?" Ellen asked when she saw the grim look on his face.

"Did you see Amy today?"

Ellen swallowed hard, unsure of where Zach was going. "Yes, I did. I came over a little after one. She wanted to talk to me."

"Did she mention if she was going somewhere
after work?"

"No. And I'm pretty sure she was planning on asking you to take her to a restaurant for dinner. What's going on?"

"She's missing."

"What do you mean *missing*?"

"Isn't it obvious what I mean?" he snapped.

"That's not necessary," Frank started.

Ellen patted his hand. "It's okay, honey. Zach, take a breath and tell me what's going on."

"I didn't mean to snap at you, Ellen." Zach looked at Frank and he nodded. "I'm just going out of my mind. I haven't heard from her all day. She had other plans for lunch, and then, when I came up here to get her when I finished at the office, she wasn't here. No one was here, actually. She hasn't called me, and she's not answering her cell phone, either."

Ellen sat down and chewed on her bottom lip for a moment. She didn't want to be the one to tell Zach about his impending fatherhood, but if something happened to Amy, or the babies, and she hadn't told him, he'd never forgive her.

"Zach," she said at last. "I know where Amy went for lunch. Sit down."

"She told you?"

"Yes, she did." Ellen looked at the men standing around. "Could you give us some privacy?" She waited until everyone else had stepped out into the hall. "She was at the doctor."

Zach's face paled. "Oh no, don't tell me..."

"Zachariah, stop and listen. She's not sick."

Zach exhaled sharply. "You're sure?"

Ellen nodded and smiled. "I'm sure."

"Then what was she doing at the doctor today?"

"She was going to tell you tonight at the restaurant. It's not really my place to say, but I'm as worried about her as you are."

"Just get on with it, Ellen. What's wrong with my wife?"

"She's pregnant Zach. With twins." And if Ellen lived another hundred years she would never forget the look on Zach's face when he heard those words. She would have laughed if he hadn't looked like he was going to pass out, and she wanted to keep an eye on him just in case he did.

"Pregnant? Twins?" He looked so stunned it was almost comical. "Why didn't she tell me? How pregnant is she?"

"A couple of months. You apparently knocked her up the first time out," she announced, enjoying seeing Zach so totally unbalanced.

"Two months?" He had a look of total bafflement on his face. "How long has she known?"

"Since the night of your reception. I confronted her about it when I found her in the house getting sick."

"*You knew*? She told you and not me.

Why?" He took a few deep breaths, and looked from the floor to Ellen. He looked so hurt just then that she almost hugged him.

"Apparently you made such a big deal about telling her you didn't want a baby with her that she was afraid to tell you. She thought you'd be angry with her and she didn't know what to do."

"Oh, no." Zach shoved a hand through his hair. "I am such an idiot."

"Exactly what I told her," Ellen said with a smile.

"I have to find her, Ellen. I have to tell her this is the best news I've ever heard. I'm going to be a father, Ellen." He jumped to his feet, then suddenly, he went perfectly still. "I'm going to be a father." His face paled and he sat down again.

"Yes, dear, I know. And those babies will survive in spite of it." Ellen patted his hand.

Zach stood and hugged Ellen. "Thank you. Sorry I was such an idiot."

"Don't worry about it, Zachariah. I'm used to it." She patted his arm. "If there's anything I can help with, just let me know."

"I will." He held the door for her and Frank as they left, and called Ron back into the room.

"Get what you can about Sam from Stan, and then run her name through every data base we've got. I want to hear something in less than thirty minutes." He started for the elevator.

"Where are you going?"

"To get a warrant for Sam's house," Zach said as he pushed the call button.

~ Seventeen ~

"Sam, it's a pretty good bet Zach is looking for me now. Someone is bound to have seen us leave the building together. He probably already has an APB out on your car. And I know he's pulling security video from the garage and everywhere else on the streets."

"I know, but this place is so out of the way, it'll be hours before he finds us. I'll be ready for him by then."

"Sam, please, just listen to me. I can help you. Zach can help you. But this is wrong and when Zach gets here, he will kill you. It won't matter to him that you're a woman, all that will matter to him will be getting to me."

"I'm not going to hurt you, Amy. You're my friend and I'd never hurt you, but this is the only way for me. I know his temper, and by the time he rescues you, he won't be able to save me."

"No, Sam. You're not saying you're *trying* to get him to kill you?"

Sam looked away. She hoped Amy would believe she was trying to commit suicide by cop, but that wasn't even close to her plan. "I'm sorry, but I'm not going to prison for what I've done. I don't know how Zach found me out, but I just can't go to prison."

"He didn't find you out, Sam. We had no idea you were the one. All Zach had come up with was dead ends where Eileen Johnson was concerned."

"But he would have eventually found me

out whether it was months, or years from now. I couldn't live with that over my head, waking up every day wondering if this was the day I'd be arrested. It'll be better this way."

"Sam, there is always another answer, a better way than this."

"Save it, Amy. Now, I'm going to take you into the bedroom so you can lie down, but I'm going to have to tie your legs so you can't get up. I have some things to get ready."

"I won't try to run, Sam. I don't want anything to happen to my babies."

She untied Amy from the chair and helped her to stand. Sam picked up her pistol and tucked it into the waistband of her jeans. Once in the bedroom she let Amy get comfortable on the bed then tied her feet together. She tied a tether from her feet to the bed and one from her hands to the headboard so Amy would be able to move but not get up.

"I'll be back in a little while. Do you want a drink of water before I go?"

Amy shook her head. "It'll just make me have to pee again."

Sam smiled weakly. "I really am happy for you and Zach," she said as she left the room and shut the door.

~ * ~

Zach rang the doorbell once. When there was no answer, he tried the handle and found it locked. "Okay, guys," he said to the team of uniformed officers with him, "break it down."

It only took one hit with the battering ram to break the lock and open the door.

Pushing the door back, he shouted,

"Police! We've got a warrant!"

No sound came from within the house. He held his service revolver up and entered the living room of Sam's house. Looking cautiously around, he motioned for the other officers to enter the house and check each room. The house was empty.

"Okay, I want every surface dusted for prints. We're also looking for any evidence that might be linked to Broom, Abernathy, or Thomas. Get some people outside and check the grounds. Turn over every rock. I don't want anything in or near this house that hasn't been touched by us before we leave here."

Zach's cell phone rang. "Yeah?" he barked.

"Zach," Ron said. "I've got records on Samantha Jane Waters, including social security, and she's dead."

"She's what?"

"Dead. She died in nineteen-sixty-eight, two weeks after she was born."

Zach took a deep breath. "And...?"

"She apparently had a California driver's license. California just happens to take a thumb-print when they issue driver's licenses, and Eileen Johnson's thumbprint matches Sam-antha's. She's the same person, Zach, no doubt about it."

Zach fought to keep his emotions under control. "Thanks. Put an APB out on her and her car. Put one out on Amy, too."

He put the phone back on his belt and took a deep breath. Blowing it out, he pushed his emotions down and let the cop take over.

By midnight he was back at the precinct with Ron. The entire team was working overtime and Zach was pacing as he waited for preliminary reports. He drank from the cup of coffee in his hand and paced some more. Finally, someone brought him a sheet of paper and he looked it over. Amy's prints had been found on a kitchen chair, the kitchen table, and on one of the doors. Zach clenched his teeth.

They had also found a burn barrel out back with residue from clothing and blankets. In the garage they had found a pocket torch, rope, and other evidence they thought they would be able to connect to the murders. It would take forensics a while but Zach was confident they would find conclusive evidence that Samantha had indeed committed three of the most heinous crimes ever recorded in New Mexico history.

"Zach, go home." Ron walked up to him. "You need to get some rest and we'll be here all night getting evidence processed. There's nothing you can do right now. So go home."

Zach shook his head. "No, I'm not going home. I'll be in my office. I can rest there and you come get me as soon as you know anything."

"I will," Ron assured him.

Zach walked down the hallway to his office and sat on the sofa. He held his face in his hands and scrubbed. He was tired, and he was more than a little worried about Amy. Stretching out on the sofa, he threw one arm over his eyes. Amy's face swam before him and the muscles in his stomach clenched. Zach felt as if his heart would burst for the love he felt for her. And from the overwhelming fear.

Never in his life had he felt such overwhelming emotions for anyone, but Amy was everything to him. He was completely in love with her and she filled every cell of his being. When he'd first met her, he'd felt lust for the first time in years. But she was nearly ten years younger than he was and he thought maybe he was going through that mid-life crisis crap he'd heard about. But as he got to know her, it wasn't just lust he'd felt.

He wanted her in his bed, that was for sure, but he also wanted her in his life on a daily basis. He didn't just want to be friends with her, didn't just want to continue having lunch with her at work, and even though he knew he'd rushed her into marrying him, he was absolutely sure he wanted her to be his wife. He hadn't wanted to give her time to think about it, time to figure out he was an old man compared to her, so he'd run roughshod over her. Now she was married to him and he'd never let her go.

Now that he thought about it, he knew he'd been sloppy too. He should've given her more time, should have given her a big church wedding. He should have been more sensitive to her, paid more attention. He was such an idiot. Hadn't he heard her in the bathroom throwing up, and when she'd told him it was just some-thing she'd eaten that disagreed with her, hadn't he just let it go at that? He balled his hands into fists and pressed them against his eyes.

She was pregnant and he hadn't even noticed. What's more, he'd told her he didn't want kids when he was just trying to protect himself from the possibility of losing her like he'd lost Stacie. He wasn't just an idiot—he was a selfish idiot. And now she was in danger and he hadn't the foggiest notion of where to look for her. Worse, he was just lying on the sofa doing nothing.

Sitting up, he raked his hands through his hair, and looked at his watch—it was nearly one in the morning. Going to his desk, he flipped open a file and scanned it until he found what he was looking for. He picked up the phone and dialed, impatiently waiting as it rang four times before the sleepy voice answered.

"Abigail? This is Detective Ellison from New Mexico. Remember, I came to your house and asked... yes, yes. I'm sorry for calling at such a late hour, but it's important. First, your sister is alive." He pulled the phone away from his ear as Abigail screamed into it, which woke her husband, who then began shouting over his wife trying to find out what had woken her and had her so upset.

"Are you sure? You're positive Detective? Is she all right? Where is she?"

"Yes, we're positive. But please calm down because I need you to think about something for me. Okay? Fine. Is there any place you can think of that Sam, er, Eileen, would go to feel safe? Anyone you can think of she would visit? A relative or friend?" He paused while Abigail thought about it.

"No. I don't know. I can't think right now, Detective. I'm sorry."

"Okay, well, you have my number if you think of anything. Don't hesitate to call me. Even if it seems like a little thing, it could be important."

"I'll call you if I think of anything at all. Thank you for letting me know about Eileen. Good night."

"You're welcome. Good night." Zach replaced the phone on its cradle and leaned back in his chair. It was a long shot but he'd been hoping maybe Abigail would have some information he could use, something maybe she hadn't thought of in years. The phone rang and he jumped, and then grabbed the receiver.

"Yeah?"

"Detective Ellison, this is Abigail."

"Yes, Abigail, did you think of something?"

"Maybe. I don't know if it will help, but my husband has a cabin out in Arizona he used to go to with his parents when he was a kid. I don't know if I ever mentioned it to Eileen since he and I had just started dating the last time Eileen came home. But I might have since he asked me to go with him for a couple of weeks that summer."

"Where is it, Abigail?"

"It's south of Flagstaff. Here, I'll let you talk to him—he'll be able to give you directions better than I can." She handed the phone to her husband and he related the directions to the cabin as Zach scribbled them onto the pad on his desk.

"Thank you, I appreciate your help."

Zach hung up the phone and grabbed his jacket as he ran out of his office. He didn't wait on the elevator, but ran down the stairs, jumping down the bottom half of each one. When he reached the first floor of the precinct he pushed the doors open on the run.

"Ron!" Zach shouted as he saw the detective in the hallway. "Come on.

"Where are we going?" Ron was putting his jacket on even as he was coming down the hall toward Zach.

"I've got a lead on Sam. I think I know where she is. Come on, we'll call it in from the car."

Both men ran out of the precinct to the parking garage and jumped into Zach's Avalanche. Zach slammed it into reverse and sped out of the garage. "We're going to a cabin owned by Sam's brother-in-law south of Flagstaff." He slung the pad of paper across the seat. "Call it in and get a hold of the Arizona State Police."

It was a good six-hour drive from Albuquerque to Flagstaff, but Zach made it in just over five hours. Pulling into the Arizona State Police headquarters, the two men ran into the building with their badges in hand. Lieutenant Grossman introduced himself and shook the two men's hands, then introduced the other officers that would be assisting in the matter.

Zach gave them the address he'd obtained from Abigail's husband. The Lieutenant laid a map on the desk and used a pencil to indicate where the cabin would be located. He mapped out a back road that would allow them access to the cabin from two different directions and continued to coordinate the plan until everyone was absolutely sure of how they would approach the scene.

"We appreciate your help," Zach said.

"This woman is wanted for three brutal murders in New Mexico and I want to take her back alive if possible. But she has a hostage, and the hostage's safety is more import-ant than the life of the suspect. No one fires a shot except on my command. I want to get them both out alive if we can." He deliberately kept the fact that the hostage was his wife. He knew they wouldn't let him take the lead in a situation to which he was so close.

Fifteen squad cars and two fully equipped S.W.A.T. team vans descended on the scene from opposite directions. Every man and woman was armed and ready, waiting on Zach's command. Holding the bullhorn to his mouth, Zach took a deep breath. He was nervous and his palms were sweaty, but he couldn't let the fact that his wife was the hostage here interfere with what he was doing now. He exhaled and pressed the trigger on the bullhorn.

"Samantha Jane Waters." His voice echoed through the mountains. "This is the police, you have no way of escape. Come out with your hands up."

There was no answer. He waited and then tried again. "Eileen Johnson, we know who you are. Come out with your hands up."

~ * ~

Amy cried as she heard Zach's voice. She felt such relief knowing he was there, would be wrapping those big arms around her and taking her home. Trying to make enough noise to be heard was impossible since Amy's mouth was covered with duct tape, and she didn't know where Sam was but she knew Sam had a gun.

Fear trickled over her spine and she tried hard to stay focused, but she was afraid for herself, for her babies, and for Samantha. She didn't know what would happen when they pressed Sam. What would happen if they fired at the house? Would Samantha fire back? The fear she felt rising in her was like a living thing as she envisioned a firefight and gas bombs being thrown into the house. She tried to calm herself, to tell herself Zach wouldn't let anything happen to her. But Zach didn't know she was pregnant either, and Amy didn't know if tear gas would hurt her babies or not.

She wiggled around. There was enough play in the tether that held her arms tied to the headboard that she could rub her arm against her mouth. She tried to get a corner of the tape to lift so she would hopefully roll it off her mouth and call out to Zach. She pushed her tongue between her teeth and lips and tried to push against the tape at the same time that she rubbed her arm across her mouth. After several attempts her tongue ached and was raw from scraping against her teeth.

Zach's voice echoed on the bullhorn again and she knew he was buying time because she was inside the cabin. But she also knew he'd have to do his job if Sam didn't respond. Amy rubbed the tape with her arm faster, pushing harder with her tongue and finally felt the little corner piece lift from her cheek. Rubbing her arm against it over and over, she gained a little ground in rolling the tape back. Then she heard Zach give one last warning that tear gas would be thrown into the building. She didn't know exactly what tear gas did, but she didn't want to find out either. Rubbing the tape harder and harder, she tried to get it off her mouth, but just then she heard glass breaking. Thinking it must be the tear gas, she was glad now that Sam had shut the bedroom door—at least she had a barrier between herself and the gas.

Hearing Sam's voice, Amy stilled in order to listen.

"I'll kill myself, Zach! Don't come any closer."

Amy rolled her eyes. Sam was acting like an idiot now and Amy knew if Sam didn't show Zach she was still alive pretty quickly, he would have no qualms about killing Sam where she stood.

Amy had managed to roll the tape back a little bit more and began rubbing her cheek against the pillow, hoping for a little more leverage against the tape. It was working slowly, and the tape began rolling back bit-by-bit. Though her cheek was raw from the rubbing and the glue from the tape was sticking against the pillow, she rubbed it over and over. Finally, it rolled back as far as her lips and she was able to use her tongue to wet the sticky back and loosen it from her skin. When it had peeled back most of the way from her lips, she began shouting Zach's name.

Her voice was weak and her throat was dry, so her voice wasn't very strong. Licking her lips, Amy tried to work up enough saliva to wet her mouth so she could swallow. Then she took another deep breath. "Zach. Zachariah." She screamed as loudly as she could. "Zachariah

Ellison!"

The bedroom door opened and Amy looked up. It was Sam. "Amy, shut up." She went to the bed and pressed the tape back over Amy's mouth, then left the bedroom and shut the door behind her. Amy heard Sam shouting from the front room.

"Zach. Can you hear me?"

"I hear you," Zach replied.

"Take your jacket off, drop your weapons, and come on in here," Sam shouted back.

"Okay, Sam."

Knowing her husband was coming inside sent even stronger emotions bolting through Amy. He was coming to rescue her, or... or to die at Sam's hands.

~ * ~

Zach set the bullhorn down and stepped out from behind the car with his hands out. He slowly removed his jacket while holding his service revolver up where Sam could see it. Then he laid it on the hood of the car. With his hands still up, he walked slowly toward the cabin.

Every cop had their weapons trained on the cabin as they watched Zach walk up the steps and disappear inside. Zach had ordered Ron Petrie to circle around the west side of the building and he now stood beside the steps that led up to the front door.

Once inside, Zach looked around the front room, allowing his eyes to adjust to the dim light. "Sam," he said quietly. There was no answer and he could see the room was empty. "Sam?" he said again.

"Zach, I'm sorry to have to do this," Sam

said from another room.

"You don't have to do anything, Samantha. We know what happened to you when you were a kid. We know about your dad and your uncles. We know why you felt you had to kill those men. We can get you all the help you need, Samantha, but you have to let me help you. You're gonna have to give me your pistol and walk out of here with me."

"I can't do that, Zach," Sam said, and Zach could tell she was crying.

"Sam, there's over fifty cops outside and the only way you'll get out of here alive is to come out with me."

"It doesn't matter anymore, Zach."

He cringed when he heard the gun go off. "Sam? Sam." Zach shouted, but there was no answer.

"Zach!" Amy screamed from somewhere deeper inside the cabin.

All thoughts of Samantha fled his mind as he ran toward the sound of Amy's voice. He saw a door and hit it with his full weight and it crashed open.

"Zach, Zach." Amy began to cry when he entered the room.

"Do you know where Sam is?"

She shook her head. Zach shouted over his shoulder to someone that the bedroom was clear, and then he came to the bed and kneeled down. "Oh, darlin'."

"Is she all right?" Ron Petrie asked.

"Get out and shut the door!" Zach yelled. "Baby, baby, baby..." He kept saying over and over while untying her hands. Amy sat up and grabbed him. He wrapped his arms around her, breathed her scent into his lungs and closed his eyes. "Let me untie your feet."

When she finally had her feet free, Zach scooped her into his arms and held her tightly. "I'm sorry, I'm sorry," she cried into his shoulder.

"Shh," he soothed her.

"No, Zach. It's my fault. I went with her. I trusted her. I didn't know. I'm sorry. I'm so sorry."

"It's not your fault, baby. You didn't do anything wrong."

"Yes, I did. I got pregnant, Zach, and I didn't tell you because I was scared, and now we're having twins, and I don't know what to do." She pushed away from him so she could look into his eyes and cupped his face in both of her hands.

"I know—Ellen told me. And I'm sorry I made you think I didn't want a baby with you. I was stupid and scared and..."

"You're not mad at me?"

"Amy, how could I be mad at you? I love you so much, and now we're having a baby. It's everything I've ever wanted."

"We're having *two* babies, Zach," Amy corrected him.

Zach took a deep breath and exhaled. "I know, it's just going to take me a minute to get used to that part."

Amy smiled and kissed him. "I love you, I love you, I love you."

"I love you, too. Let's get out of here." He took her by the hand and led her toward the door. Just as he reached for the door handle the first blast blew it off its hinges, pushing Zach backward against Amy. They landed against the bed with the door on top of them.

Zach shoved the door off his chest and rolled off of Amy. Grabbing her around the waist, he pulled her down on the floor behind the bed and lay on top of her. The second blast shook the cabin off its foundation and most of the roof flew off. Zach looked around, could smell the smoke and see flames rising in front of and above him. The frame of the bed blocked the only window in the room, so he shoved Amy up against the wall near the head of the bed.

"Stay right there," he ordered.

Standing, he grabbed the headboard with one hand and the bottom of the bed frame with the other, and heaved it out of the way. Black smoke was filling the room quickly and hot flames rapidly followed. Zach turned the latch on the window and pushed up on the wooden frame but it didn't budge. He pushed again, but it still didn't budge, so he turned his head and put his elbow through the pane, breaking the window out. Then he pulled a pillow off the bed, ripped the case from it and wrapped it around his hand to protect it from the shards of glass that protruded from the frame. He ran his hand around the frame and knocked the rest of the glass to the ground.

"Come on," he said and grabbed Amy's arm and hoisted her up until she was halfway through the window and then pushed her the rest of the way through. Just as he was about to push himself up, another blast rocked the house and the last thing he remembered was the hot *whoosh* of air that pushed him backwards through the wall. He had the sensation of falling, of flying, of spinning through the air, and then there was only darkness.

~ * ~

Amy screamed when Zach's head disappeared from the window as she looked up from the ground where she'd landed. The blast of heat and flying debris covered her as she crawled on her hands and knees trying to get to safety.

"Zach! Zach!" She screamed his name over and over. Then she felt herself being lifted from the ground as two Arizona officers carried her through the debris that had once been the cabin and placed her on a gurney from an ambulance.

"Zach!" she screamed again.

"It's okay, it's okay," a female paramedic told her. "Are you hurt anywhere else?"

Amy looked at the woman, confused by what she was asking her. "What?"

"Do you hurt anywhere else?" She wrapped a blood pressure cuff around Amy's arm and pumped it up.

Amy looked down and saw blood but didn't know where it was coming from. "Where's Zach? Where's my husband?"

"I don't know," the woman said as she wrote on a piece of paper attached to the clipboard. "I just want to take care of you right now. Are you on medication? Anything I should know about you?"

Amy nodded. "I'm pregnant with twins."

The woman smiled. "Congratulations. How far along are you?"

"Two months." Amy looked past the woman, searching for Zach among the people milling around the debris.

"I need you to lie back on the stretcher. We're going to take you to the hospital and let a doctor look at you. I think your wounds are pretty superficial but you'll need a few stitches. And since you're pregnant, we need a doctor to take a listen and make sure your babies are fine, too."

Amy grabbed the woman's arm. "My babies. You think something's wrong with them?"

"No, honey, I don't. But I'm not a doctor, and I know we'd both feel better if we let one tell us all three of you are all right. You've got some pretty nasty cuts, and I think you could use some stitches, but I don't think you have any really serious injuries."

"Okay, but will you try to find out where my husband is?"

"Sure. You just relax." The woman climbed out of the ambulance and walked out of Amy's line of sight. She was gone a few minutes and when she returned, she said, "Okay, we're going to get you to the hospital now."

"What about my husband? Where is he?"

"He's on his way to the hospital, but I don't know anything about his condition. You'll be able to find out more when we get there."

The trip to the hospital took a lot longer than Amy thought it would. When they finally arrived, she could see another ambulance in the emergency bay beside them. Doctors and nurses surrounding the gurney blocked her view and she couldn't see who was on the stretcher. Amy felt her heart in her throat and a cold wave of fear swept over her.

"Is that Zach?" she whispered.

"I really don't know," a paramedic said as they wheeled her into the emergency room.

~ Eighteen ~

The breeze blew softly across the cemetery as the hearse made its way slowly along the paved road to the burial site. A long line of vehicles escorted by policemen on motorcycles followed it. Pallbearers stood in dress blues as the back of the hearse opened to reveal the shiny black coffin with bright, shiny brass hand railings. The pallbearers stood at attention, then reached for the casket with white-gloved hands and brought the coffin into the sunlight. Lifting the casket onto their shoulders, they carried it to the burial area where a green canopy had been placed over the freshly dug grave. Mourners followed slowly behind, with most of the police department present. Only those who were absolutely essential to the skeleton crew still on duty were absent.

When they had all made their way to the gravesite, the police honor guard took their positions with rifles in hand for the twenty-one-gun salute that would come later. The police chaplain took his place at the head of the coffin, looking somberly to his left where family members sat. Amy glanced up at the chaplain, then back at the casket. She held a handkerchief in her hand, and even though she wore sunglasses, it was easy to see that she'd been crying.

Zach put his arm around her. The other one was in a cast and sling next to his body. There were stitches across one cheekbone, and his cracked ribs were wrapped tightly to make it easier for him to move. A cane leaned against his leg and the doctor said he'd have to use it even after his leg healed from being impaled by a piece of wood from the exploding cabin. There would be no permanent physical damage, but as he looked around him, Zach couldn't help but wonder just how severe the psychological damage would be.

Amy looked up at Zach and smiled weakly, then she looked over at Leslie Petrie who sat holding her five-year-old daughter, Katie, with dry eyes. Ten-year-old Anthony sat beside his mother and sister staring at the black coffin that held his father's body. Amy's heart constricted in her chest as she looked at Ron's wife who would now be raising his children alone. She felt guilty because she had been so relieved Zach was alive, and because in some strange way, she felt it was her fault that Ron had died.

When the service was over, they stood and hugged Leslie and Katie. Zach shook hands with Anthony and told him if he ever needed anything to call him. Leslie thanked everyone, and then walked back to the waiting cars. Family and those closest to Ron, accompanied Leslie back to the house she and Ron bought right after they had married. There was plenty of food and drink and music for the wake. Leslie was Irish and had a large family that took over the place, and it soon looked like a celebration. When the crowd finally began to thin out, Zach and Amy hugged Leslie again and made her promise to call if she needed anything.

They rode home in silence, and Earl bounded out to greet them when they pulled up beside the house. "Hey, Earl, I guess you want a cookie, huh?" Zach scratched the dog's head and led him into the laundry room as he opened the door for Amy. He got a dog biscuit from the shelf above the washing machine and then hobbled back out onto the porch with Earl nearly tripping him.

"Be a gentleman," he said and the dog sat obediently. He gave Earl the treat and scratched him again. "Good dog."

Zach looked out across the land he owned and thought how good it was to have things simple and how simple things stayed the same—the land, the cows, Earl eating a biscuit on the lawn. Yeah, it was the simple things that made life worth living, and those were the things that would get Leslie Petrie through the days, weeks, and months ahead. Raising her children, the routine that life demanded, those things would get her through. And he and Amy would be there when she didn't feel like she could face even the most mundane things of life.

Zach went inside and found Amy curled up on the bed crying. Lying down beside her, he held her close with his good arm. He didn't speak, he just let her climb halfway on top of him, bury her face in his neck, and cry her eyes out. When she finally calmed down, he rubbed the pad of his thumb across her cheek and wiped the tears there. He hated seeing her in such a state, but ever since they had returned from Arizona, she had been very emotional and cried often. Zach wondered if it would hurt the babies and had even called the doctor to find out.

"It's okay, darlin'," Zach soothed her.

"We'll help out Leslie as much as we can, but she has a big family that will be there for her. And Ron's family, too."

"I know," she sniffled. "Do you think it's wrong I feel so much relief it wasn't you? I just keep thinking I shouldn't feel so happy about it."

"It's natural you'd feel guilty for being happy you're not going through what Leslie is right now. You know how easily it could've been Ron and me both that were buried today. I feel the same way. I'm happy because I'm alive and guilty because it was Ron and not me. It's just human nature. I've seen it so many times since I became a cop, but you have every right to be happy your husband is alive. I know your husband is."

"It could've been so different, Zach..."

Zach put a finger over her lips. "It wasn't, so don't go there. I'm just glad it wasn't worse than it was. The Arizona police lost four good officers, and we lost one. That's enough casualties for any police force. All of those families are grieving just like we are, and all of them will have to find their own way through the grief. I am just grateful you weren't killed in the process, and you easily could have been." He held her then, shut his eyes and willed the thought away. "But it didn't happen that way, and we're both fine, and our baby is fine."

"Babies," Amy corrected him.

"Our *babies* are fine," he said and smiled at her.

"And what about Sam?"

"I don't know. We have to wait and see what they come up with when they get done sifting through the ashes. I don't think she was still there. She wasn't anywhere in the cabin that I could see when I was trying to find you. I don't know if she killed herself, or if she just wanted us to think she had. And the bombs were on timers, so she could have slipped out of the cabin somehow after she fired the shot to make me think she'd shot herself, or you. So, for now, she's presumed alive and well, and there's a nationwide manhunt for her too. We'll find her if she's alive."

"She talked like she wanted to die—at least that's what I thought she was saying. She wasn't going to go to prison willingly, that's for sure. How could I work with her every day and not know?"

"Sweetie, it happens all the time. How many times do the neighbors of serial killers say how nice a neighbor they were, how quiet they were, how they would've never guessed what the person really was? People are very good at hiding who they really are from the rest of the world."

~ Nineteen ~

Christmas morning came and Amy was up early getting the turkey ready for the oven. Her stomach was so big she had to stand sideways at the kitchen sink to reach the taps. Her ankles were swollen, but she couldn't tell because it had been months since she'd seen her own feet. Her back ached and her stomach seemed to just keep getting bigger and bigger. The twins weren't due for another month, but Amy was praying for it to go by quickly. She felt as if she'd been pregnant forever, and she'd been fantasizing about ways she'd heard of to induce labor.

She'd been told drinking castor oil would cause labor, and riding over bumpy roads would cause it, and that sex was a sure fire guarantee. While the first two didn't sound too appealing, the third had been just up her alley. Her hormones had been out of control and she couldn't get enough sex. She was just so bulky now that it was almost impossible to find a comfortable position. She would do anything at this point to get this party going. She felt as if she had been pregnant for at least a year already and was beginning to think it was a permanent condition.

"What are you doing?" Zach asked as he walked toward her. He'd stood watching her as she prepared the turkey for the oven and thought how beautiful she looked. And the larger her stomach grew, the more beautiful she was to him. She was carrying his baby. No, he corrected himself, she was carrying *two* of his babies, and there was nothing more beautiful than that.

She turned to see Zach walk into the kitchen with just a pair of jeans pulled up and left unbuttoned, and she felt that familiar pull within her as she looked over his naked chest. They were still newlyweds, yet Amy felt as if they had always been together, and she couldn't imagine her life without him. And now they were just a few short weeks away from becoming parents together and as much as that frightened her, it also thrilled her.

He kissed her. "Merry Christmas." Then he laid a brightly wrapped gift on the counter.

"What is this?"

"Unwrap it and see." He rubbed his hands over her stomach, then lifted her blouse and kissed her bare belly. It still amazed him that as small as she was she could actually stretch to the size she was now and not just split right in half.

Amy washed her hands and dried them with a paper towel, then picked up the gift and unwrapped it to reveal a slim velvet box. Looking at Zach with bright eyes, she carefully lifted the lid. The gold and diamond bracelet winked at her.

"Oh Zach, it's beautiful. Thank you so much." She hugged him and lifted her lips to his. "Put it on me," she said and held her hand out.

He took the bracelet and wrapped it around her wrist and latched the clasp. "See?" He pointed to spaces on the bracelet. "After the babies are born you can have their birth stone placed in it as well, or you can just leave like it is."

"Oh, that's so perfect." A tear slid down

her cheek. "You are the most... oow... oh my..."

"Amy? What's wrong?" Zach felt fear and panic rising in him as he saw anguish and pain shoot across her face.

She bent forward and clutched her stomach. "Call the doctor, Zach. Now."

~ * ~

Amy lay in the hospital bed and watched Zach pace the floor as the nurse prepped her for the delivery room. An I.V. had been placed in her arm and the infant heart monitor echoed the heartbeats of their babies. Amy knew Ellen and Frank were in the waiting room, as were a few people from the D.A.'s office. Pete was also there. Since Ron's death, Zach and Pete's bond had grown ever closer. Zach had called Amy's parents to let them know they were about to become grandparents, and they were now waiting impatiently by the phone for the next call.

Suddenly, Amy felt something warm and wet against her flesh. "What was that?"

"What?" Zach went to her side.

The nurse laughed. "Your water just broke. Looks like you're getting yourself Christmas babies after all. I need to let the doctor know so she can check you again. I'll be right back."

"Are you scared?" Zach smoothed her hair away from her face.

Amy nodded. "A little bit. I just don't know what it's like. I've seen all the videos and talked to other women, but I still don't know what it's really going to feel like and that makes me nervous. I'm afraid I won't be able to handle it, that the pain will be too much."

"I'll be right beside you. You can hang on to me, squeeze my hand, cuss me out—I don't care. And if it is too bad, you let the doctor know, and she can give you something."

Zach leaned down and kissed his wife, then smiled gently as he caressed her face, and Amy knew he would have gone through it for her if he could have.

"Okay, Amy," Dr. Freeman said as she came into the room. "How're you doing, Zach? Hanging in there?" When Zach nodded, she continued. "Good. Now Amy, I'm going to check your cervix and see how much you've progressed."

She slid gloves over her hands and the nurse squeezed lubricant onto the fingers of one hand.

"Okay, this may be a little uncomfortable, but it won't hurt." She inserted her fingers and felt Amy's cervix, then pulled her hand out and looked at the blood on the fingers of the glove.

"Is that normal?" Zach asked, just a little alarmed to see his wife's blood.

"It sure is and, Amy, you're dilated to nine centimeters. Let's get you into the delivery room before the babies decide to come right here."

"So fast?" Amy looked at Zach and then back at the doctor. "I haven't even had any real pain."

"It happens that way sometimes. Not usually with the first pregnancy, but it's not unheard of. And there will be enough pain and work in the next hour or so that you'll be happy you didn't lay here in labor for hours and hours."

They wheeled her into the delivery room and one of the nurses helped Zach get into a gown and mask. Amy felt just a little embarrassed when her legs were put into the stirrups and left her bare for all to see. But when the first real contraction ripped through her, she forgot all about being embarrassed. Dr. Freeman slipped her fingers inside Amy again and felt through the contraction.

"You're completely dilated and one-hundred percent effaced. I want you to push with the next contraction."

Less than a minute later Amy began pushing with all her might. The contractions came so rapidly, and she pushed so fiercely, the doctor told her to relax and pant through the next one. The first baby's head was already out and the doctor suctioned the tiny nose and mouth. With the next contraction, the baby screamed and plopped out onto the sterile blue cloth in the doctor's waiting hands.

"It's a boy," she announced and went about clamping the cord that Zach cut, and the baby was laid on Amy's chest. A nurse covered the baby with a warm blanket and after Amy and Zach had both kissed their new son, she took him to be weighed and measured.

"Here comes another one," Amy said and began to push.

"Okay, I see a head. One more push and then pant through it just like the last one, Amy," Doctor Freeman instructed. The baby began to scream before the doctor could finish suctioning the nose and mouth. "Here's your troublemaker," the doctor laughed and told Amy to push again. "Another boy."

Amy looked at the red-faced baby squalling on her chest and burst into tears as she kissed him. "Zach, we've got sons."

"Yeah." Zach choked on the lump in his throat and kissed the baby's wet head.

"Oh, oh... I'm having another contraction," Amy screamed.

"It's just to expel the placenta," the doctor explained.

"I don't think so," Amy cried. "It hurts. And I have to push."

Dr. Freeman placed two fingers inside of Amy and then looked up at Zach. "Now *this* has never happened to me before. There's another baby."

Zach's mouth fell open as Amy began to push.

"Push, Amy, push." Dr. Freeman encouraged. "Okay, now pant through it." She suctioned the baby's mouth and nose and the room soon filled with a shrill scream as the baby took its first breath.

"Okay, one more good push, Amy. That's it. And we have a girl."

Zach openly wept. Amy cried as well when the baby girl was placed on her chest.

"Oh Zach, can you believe this? Oh my gosh, Zach, we have *three* babies." She touched the baby's cheek and kissed her head. She looked at the doctor and asked, "Are they all right? They're early."

"They aren't all that early for triplets. They all look and sound perfectly fine to me. Now how about we get you taken care of? Then

you'll be able to hold them and get started
nursing."

~ * ~

Zach and Amy stood in the nursery of their
home and looked at their three babies. They'd
named the boys Mathew and Michael, and their
baby girl was named Mary after Zach's grand-
mother who had raised him. They'd only been
expecting two children so there were only two
cribs. For now all three babies were in one crib,
but later as they grew larger and became more
active, they'd be moved to their own cribs.

Friends and family had been dropping in to
help with feedings, baths, and diapering. Gifts
had been coming in as well, and the new parents
really had no idea where they were going to put
everything.

"I guess we'll have to add on to the
house," Zach said, wrapping an arm around
Amy's shoulders.

"Really? That would be wonderful. I've got
this whole blueprint in my mind of what it will
look like. I just worry about the cost." Amy had
decided she wasn't going to go back to work for
quite some time, if ever. She wanted to be a
stay-at-home mom and Zach was happy with the
idea.

"I think we can handle it."

"I want to sell my house, Zach. Now don't
argue, it's mine to do with as I please, and the
couple who are renting it have asked a few times
about buying, so I'm going to sell it to them."

"If you want to, then do it," Zach said
with a shrug.

"We can use the money to build the

addition to the house," she added.

"Amy..." Zach started. He was a modern man in a lot of ways, but taking care of his wife and children was his responsibility, and he took it seriously. Amy's money was hers to do with as she pleased, and he didn't expect her to support them. That was his job.

"No, Zach, it's ours. All of it. The house, babies, money, the bills too. It's as much my responsibility as it is yours. And I want to do this."

Kissing her, he said, "If it's what you want."

He knew he would never deny her anything, and he knew he would love her for the rest of his life. He'd never known such peace, and he'd never known a love like this. Looking at his wife and the children they'd made caused his heart to swell with love. This was all he'd ever wanted in life, and more than he ever hoped to have. He knew he was a blessed man, and that too, amazed him.

Standing behind Amy, Zach wrapped his arms around her, and nuzzled her hair, inhaling the fresh fragrance he'd come to recognize as hers alone. He felt heat rising within him, spreading to his stomach and into his loins. He bent and kissed the back of her neck.

"What do you think you're doing there, Ellison?"

"Trying to convince my wife to come into the bedroom with me," he said and nibbled her ear.

"What, triplets aren't enough for you?" He stopped cold and she laughed. "Well, it looks like

I've found a way to turn you off."

He grinned. "You think so?" Grabbing her, he swung her into his arms, and carried her to the bedroom. Laying her down, he kissed her gently, and told her, "I love you, Amy."

"I love you, too, Zach."

He kissed her throat as his fingers worked the buttons on her blouse. He trailed a finger along her skin, following it with his tongue. She moaned and sank her fingers into his thick hair, raking her nails over his scalp, as he pushed her shirt back, all three babies began to cry and Amy laughed.

Zach shut his eyes and dropped his head to her stomach. "We'll never make love again, will we?"

Amy laughed. "I would never say never darling, just not for the next eighteen years or so."

He growled and stood. Offering a hand, he pulled Amy to her feet. She stood on tiptoes and kissed him.

"Come on, our children are calling us."

Hand in hand, they went back into the nursery, and as Amy settled into the rocking chair, she held two of the babies football style and nursed them while Zach rocked the third one gently in his arms. He smiled at the sight of his wife with his children in her arms, and he sighed. This was his life and he loved everything about it.

~ Epilogue ~

"Zach, do you think we'll ever see Sam again?"

"I don't know, Amy. There are warrants out for her everywhere, so she'll never be able to cross the border back into the U.S. again. But I think, eventually, she will be caught."

"It's been nearly three years." Amy dumped another load of laundry into the washing machine and turned the knobs. Three two year olds made for a lot of work and even more laundry than Amy had ever imagined.

"I know, but she'll make a mistake. Eventually, she'll want to come home. She'll want to come back here, come back to what is familiar, what she knows." Zach sorted the rest of the laundry into separate baskets and lined them up against the wall behind Amy. "There," he announced. "Laundry's all ready to go." He pulled Amy to him and kissed her. "Don't worry about Sam, darlin', she won't ever hurt you again."

"No, I'm not worried about that, Zach. She never meant to hurt me. I know she was just desperate. You may not believe it, but she was my friend and I don't hold a grudge."

Zach shook his head. "I do. She could have killed you, Amy. She could have killed our children. I will never forgive her for that, not ever."

"You're a cop through and through, my love," she said as she smiled and kissed him gently. "Oops, that's my cue," she said grinning, and headed for the bedroom where she had heard the triplets waking up from their nap. "Come on, Daddy, you can help me wrestle them into submission."

Zach scooped up his daughter and one of his boys, then kissed his other son as he sat on the edge of the bed to help Amy change and dress the triplets and get them ready for lunch. He played with two of them while Amy dressed a third, then switched with her until they were all ready. He was amazed at how Amy took care of everyone, including him, without ever missing a beat.

She managed to cook, clean, and care for triplets all day while he was at work and only had a housekeeper come in twice a week to help her out. He watched her fix lunch for everyone while he kept the triplets occupied in their high chairs. He didn't know how she did it now, especially since her stomach grew larger with the impending arrival of their newest addition, he didn't know why he had ever agreed to have another baby.

~ * ~

Waking up early the next morning, Zach slid quietly out of bed and into the triplet's room. It had become his morning routine to rise before Amy, get the triplets changed and feed them their breakfast before he went to work. He enjoyed the time alone with them and now that they were running everywhere, they accompanied him out to the barn each morning. As their family had grown, so had the animals on the ranch. What had started out as a few head of cattle and a couple of horses, now included ponies for each of the triplets, a coop full of laying hens, rabbits, ducks and geese, but the favorite animal of course was Earl. Each of the triplets carried a doggie biscuit outside and fed Earl, then hugged him and he rolled over on his back to let them scratch his tummy.

When all four returned to the house, Amy had coffee ready and was sitting at the kitchen table with a cup in her hand. She smiled when her two sons and daughter ran to her with flowers they had picked in their chubby little hands. She kissed each one as she took the flowers and put them in a vase on the table that held more flowers from mornings past.

Zach showered quickly and got ready to go to work. "I'll see you all this evening," he said and kissed his children and wife good-bye. "You three help Mommy today, okay?"

Amy fell easily into her morning routine and when it was finally time for the triplets' nap, she used the time to shower and dress. Afterward, she put a roast into the crockpot so it would be ready when Zach got home. She went into the laundry room and transferred a load from the washer to the dryer and started another load, and then she heard Earl begin to bark, followed by a horn honking.

Amy went out the back door and took a package from the UPS man and thanked him with a smile. Back inside, she opened the small box and found three silver spoons. She smiled as she looked at each one. Then she picked up the note and unfolded the paper. It read:

For the little princess and the two princes. Glad you are okay. All of you. Sorry for everything. S.

Sitting down slowly, Amy felt suddenly weak in the knees as she read the note over and over. It was from Samantha—she was alive and apparently fine. Amy couldn't believe Sam would contact her like this, and while she felt relieved that Sam was alive and well, a chill ran up her spine. Amy looked at the box but the return address given was the District Attorney's office.

Taking a breath, she blew it out. No, she wasn't afraid Sam was back, and she wasn't afraid Sam was coming after her. Samantha was apologizing the only way she could, though Amy knew Zach wouldn't see it that way. She put the silver spoons back into the box with the note and folded the lid back down. She would think about it and decide what to tell Zach when he got home.

The rest of the day was routine, or at least as routine as life with triplets ever got. Amy cared for her children and used what spare time she had cleaning up after them. When Zach finally got home that evening Amy decided she wouldn't tell him right away about the gift Sam had sent—no reason to upset his good mood. He kissed her and picked up all three children at once and then fell onto the floor with them and wrestled noisily. They screamed and giggled and squealed while Zach laughed and tickled them and Amy finished getting supper ready. After supper Zach bathed the triplets while Amy cleaned the kitchen, and then they read a bedtime story together and tucked the three into their beds and kissed them goodnight.

"Alone at last," Zach sighed with a grin and pulled Amy to him as they sat on the sofa.

"Would you like something to drink?"

"A glass of juice would be good. And if you wanted to rub my feet I wouldn't argue," she called after him as he disappeared into the kitchen.

Zach returned with the juice and the box she'd received earlier that day. "What's this?"

"Oh" Amy said and shrugged as she took the box. "It came today." She opened the box and handed him the three spoons.

"Cute," Zach said as he looked at them and handed them back to her. "Who sent them?"

"They were just a gift," she said with a yawn and stretched. "Rub my feet, *please*."

Zach pulled her legs onto his lap and began massaging her feet. "Better?"

"Not yet, keep going," she mumbled.

"So who sent the spoons?"

"Come on, Detective. It's just a gift."

"From...?"

Amy inhaled, then exhaled and moaned. "Sam," she finally said with a sigh.

Zach's hands stilled as he looked at her. "Sam? Samantha Waters?"

"Mmm, hmm." Amy kept moaning, her eyes closed as she waited for the explosion.

"Amy Lynn, what are you thinking? You should have called me immediately."

"Zach, there's no reason to get upset, and no reason to talk to me like that."

Zach took her by the wrists and pulled her to a sitting position. "Amy... " he started.

"Come on Zach, I didn't call you because of this. You would have rushed home with more cops following you. This would have been a crime scene, with pictures and fingerprints being taken and the note would've been... "

"There's a note? Where is it, Amy?"

Amy started laughing. "Ellison, you are a piece of work." She fell backwards onto the sofa, still laughing. "It's in the box," she said, but he already had the box in his hands.

Zach read the note several times, carefully holding the very edges so he wouldn't ruin any fingerprints that might be present. "You could have said something," he said with exasperation evident in his voice.

"Look, Zach, I don't want you to turn this into an investigation. Just let it be, okay? Just forget about it and let it be."

Zach said nothing for a long while. "Amy, I have a job to do. Samantha is wanted for murder—not just murder but the murder of cops, the murder of my best friend. She left his son fatherless, his wife without a husband, not to mention the families of the troopers she killed in Arizona. Even if I wanted to let it be, I can't. And it's not just my job—it's you and the kids, Amy. You four, five—" He rubbed a protective hand over her stomach, "—are the priorities in my life. You have to understand that, you have to know I will do anything to protect you... even if I wasn't a cop."

Amy sighed again. She knew all of that, and it was only one of the many things about him that she loved. She reached for him and he pulled her onto his lap as she wrapped her arms around his neck. "I know, Zach. It's why I love you. I just don't want you going after her. And for the same reasons. Here, I know we are all safe. She won't come back here. I just know it. But she almost killed you too, Zach, and the thought of being a widow, of our kids being fatherless like Ron's family just scares me so much."

"I know," he whispered and brushed hair from her face. He kissed her eyes, kissed her mouth gently. She molded herself to him, wrapped her fingers in his hair and pressed her mouth to his in a deep, seductive kiss. When she broke the kiss, she remained in his arms.

"Zach," she said looking into his eyes. "Make love to me tonight and be a cop tomorrow."

He answered her with another kiss and carried her to their room.

About the Author

Marie McGaha lives in SE Oklahoma in the Kiamichi Wilderness, with her husband, Nathan. The couple is members of The Patriot Guard Riders, and Nathan is the captain of 18Wheels Chapter SE580 and Marie is the chapter chaplain.

Besides riding motorcycles, Marie cares for a plethora of rescued animals, and loves spoiling her grandchildren. When she has the chance, she also runs Dancing With Bear Publishing, writes fiction and non-fiction, Christian books, and sweet romance. Marie's most recent endeavor is to fulfill a life-long dream of owning her own shoe store and designing shoes, and she has just realized that dream!

www.mariemcgaha.com
www.girlsgotgrit.com
FB @AuthorMarieMcGaha
Twitter /Marie_McGaha